JAMES ALDERDICE

FURY Copyright 2019 James Alderdice

Cover by J Caleb Design https://www.jcalebdesign.com/

Map by Anna Stansfield

http://artofannastansfield.blogspot.com/

Digital formatting by: Hershel Burnside

All rights reserved. Without limiting the rights under copyright reserved above, no part of this publication may be reproduced, stored in or introduced into a retrieval system, or transmitted, in any form, or by any means (electronic, mechanical, photocopying, recording, or otherwise) without the prior written permission of both the copyright owners and the above publisher of this book.

LOST REALMS PRESS

CHAPTERS

† † †

PROLOGUE: THE DRAGON AWAKES 1
1. LEGEND OF THE WYRM'S TOOTH 7
2. THE DISAGREEMENT 20
3. ENCOUNTER IN THE FOREST 30
4. ROLL THE BONES 38
5. THE NIGHT STALKER 47
6. THE RABBITS DEN 54
7. SOUR WELCOMES 62
8. LAY OF THE LAND 75
9. DEMANDS AND THREATS 86
10. THE DOOM LADEN TRAIL 92
11. SONG OF TREACHERY 102
12. MORALS AND DOGMA 113
13. DRUM AND FANG 121
14. REMEMBER THE TUNE 134
15. ARMED TO THE TEETH 144
16. TO THE MARSH 157
17. A MOTHERS VENGEANCE 163
18. IN THE DEPTHS OF A BLACK WELL 169
19. THE HOARD 176
20. RETURN OF THE KING 182
EPILOGUE: TO THE CROWN 190

THE WORLD OF THE USURPER KING

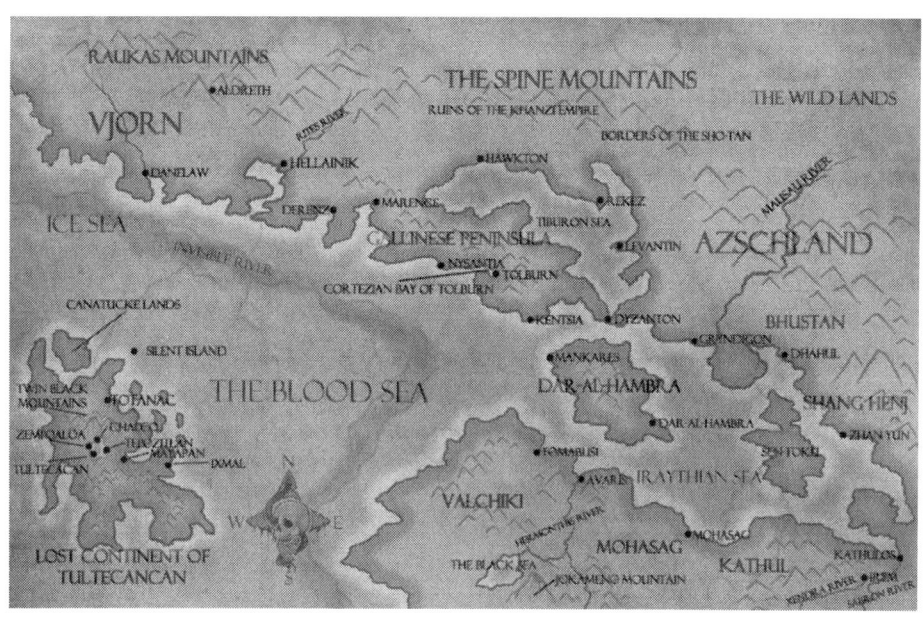

For Adam "The Brometheus"

FURY 🗡 🗡 🗡 JAMES ALDERDICE

PROLOGUE: THE DRAGON AWAKES

Darkness had taken her and when she awoke, crisp orange danced before her eyes not a hands breadth away. Fires crackled along the ground, burning thatch from a fallen roof. A blackened hand lay singed beside the greedy blaze, the unknown body it belonged to crushed by the fallen timbers. Was it one of her hand maids? Probably.

The pitiful wailing of pain and sadness carried over the grim scene. A fetid reek pervaded the courtyard amidst the death and destruction. Blood was splattered crimson across the snow like sorrow. Her body was freezing from lying in snow and ice but also burnt from being too near the devouring flames of the ruined palace.

She crawled free of the wreckage which attempted to trap her legs—luckily nothing felt broken. The fallen timbers had cracked her skull and a small amount of blood in dried rivulets caught her long black hair and pasted it down her pale face. Mind reeling, she cast about for anyone living, and then the memory of the horrific attack came, and she spun, hunting for the architect of this doom—the dragon.

Finding no sign of the horrific beast she hurried on, hunting for someone, anyone, still alive.

Rancid smoke curled over her shoulders, hiding the living from her gaze like wraiths in the mist. Daring not to speak aloud for fear of the monster, she stepped carefully feeling her way through the palpable gloom.

She heard men grunting a short distance away and ran toward them through the wheeling smoke. Passing through the amorphous veil she recognized the voice of the lord of the ruined palace. "Father?"

"I am here, daughter! Thank the gods you live!" said her father. "Let me look at you." He ran stern hands over her face and wiped away at the caked blood. "Any other wounds?"

She felt at her torn gown. Her legs were badly bruised, she was sure, but nothing felt broken or cut. "I don't think so. Where is mother?"

Her father shook his head, lips downturned into a frown, then clutched her to his breast. They held each other tight and wept.

"Lord Hoskuld, I have her free," spoke one the men, as they dragged the body of his lady from beneath the ruins of a wall.

Her father's embrace intensified, not allowing her to look upon the broken visage of her mother. "You don't need to see this," he said. "Always remember her as she was, a beautiful queen, your mother."

She struggled to look one last time, but he was so much stronger and kept her pressed tight against his cold armor.

FURY † † † JAMES ALDERDICE

"Bors," Hoskuld ordered his headman, "Cover my lady and take her away. We must see to the rest of the dead."

"Let me at least touch her hand," she said, "one last time."

Hoskuld, with tears streaming down his own lined face, gazed upon his daughter and nodded.

She caressed the cold dead hand then gripped it tight. Tears fell, nearly blinding her as she swore, "Damn this dragon from hell! May Votan blight your bones!"

"Take my daughter to the hall and see that someone, a maid, cares for her bruises and that crack on the skull," ordered Hoskuld.

She was carried away by one of the men at arms and then fell into a swoon and slept, dreaming mad dreams where giant shapes lurked in the dim fog and great jaws snapped ominously.

† † †

That evening, she knelt beside the shrine of Votan, behind the ruined palace. She placed small incense burners before the twin pillars of Votan and his Queen Celene. Smoke surrounded her everywhere she went. Black plumes still rose from fires trapped beneath tumbled monoliths that the workmen could not reach and extinguish.

She had been kneeling in front of the shrine almost all day. It was a massive block of stone with incredible detail carved upon the two pillars joined by a small arch above. It had been crafted long ago, when men worked intricate fashion beyond the skill they possessed today. It was their people's best connection to the past and their ancestors, so it was venerated by most, but not all.

Her skeptical father, Hoskuld, walked up behind her. "Praying?"

"Why did it come? Why take mother and all the rest?"

Hoskuld shrugged. "If your mother would have ever had a choice in the matter, she would have wanted you to live."

"Why? My life is worth no more than anyone else's," she said.

"No parent would agree to that."

She looked at him with tears streaming down her face.

"We all want answers," he said, "but in this life, sometimes only the gods know that riddle and they will not share it with those of us that are still trapped in the flesh."

"You never pray," she said accusingly. "So how can you know?"

"I've never needed to. Not sure there is any point in starting now," he said, coldly. He cast a wistful look at his destroyed palace.

"I want answers," she said, wiping away the tears. "Don't you?"

Hoskuld cast his arms about in despair. "Who knows why a dragon does what a dragon does, or why the gods allow them to afflict us so. If we really are their children, why pain us like this?" He leaned against the shrine and ran a hand along the carved face of Votan. "Once, perhaps, I believed in divine justice, but not anymore. This life is pain. We are but a game of dice to the gods," he said softly. "At best they laugh at our struggles."

"Mother didn't believe that."

"Perhaps she didn't." He set a hand on her shoulder.

"But that is not why I am here," she said.

"Why are you here then? Praying at the shrine of Votan. It will be dark soon, and we must find shelter for the night. The wise man says the dragon will be back with the coming darkness."

She stood, her eyes ablaze. "I want answers, but most of all I want revenge upon the dragon. I have been here all day praying and giving libations to the gods that they will send the killer of souls to destroy the monster!"

Hoskuld looked with surprise upon his daughter. She was a full-grown woman now, beautiful as a night filled with stars and the full glory of the moon. Until yesterday evening, all his thoughts for her had been on finding a worthy husband and soon, but the dragon changed everything. He and his men could not slay the beast, they couldn't even prevent it from destroying his meager palace and taking his wife and dozens of other souls away. So much death. But beyond that, he never expected this bold and vengeful determination to cross her face. This was trouble, and he didn't wish to lose a daughter along with his wife.

"And if the gods do not hear our prayers? What then?" he said, simply.

She looked at him and wiped away the tears. "They will hear my curses."

"Listen to me," he shouted, taking her by the shoulders. "The dead are gone! Ash on the wind! I won't have you become what I am! You're going away before any more death and bitterness touches you!"

"You can't make me leave. This is my home!"

"I am lord of Finnsburg, and you will go if I have to tie you up and bind you to a horse! I won't debate this with you. You're going!"

"No!"

"Pack your personal items, you will leave in the morning!"

"No, I won't! This is my home! My land!"

He raised his hand as if to strike her, but she only stuck out her chin to claim the slap, to feel the pain on her face to match a broken heart.

"You will go, if I have to have Bors carry you on his back! Argh!" he cried in anger and threw down his hands before doing something else he might regret. He reached into a pocket. "Take this. It was your mothers." He held out a great red jewel on a chain. She took it without looking at it. He then strode away fuming.

The red glare of the setting sun over the mountains fit her mood. She saw crimson everywhere.

Turning back to the shrine of Votan, she looked upon the carven image of the stormy bearded god, the lines of his face hewn deep into the pillar. It was all things at once, stern and unfeeling, cold and vengeful. It looked like her father. "He heard me. He knows my words and so do you. Votan, send a man to slay the dragon. A man beyond all others who is a killer of souls and will save my people and my land."

FURY \ \ \ JAMES ALDERDICE
1. LEGEND OF THE WYRM'S TOOTH

The sloop was half swamped and limped into the bay of a coastal village halfway between Danelaw and Hellaink. The skipper dared not take his ship further on for fear of her going down, not to mention he wished to be rid of his dangerous passengers as soon as look upon them. They were fighting men that was sure, big bold men yet pantherish and quick. He had his suspicions but kept that to himself. The weather was a simpler reason to be rid of them.

Slate grey skies overhead promised rain soon but for now there was only the tang of the sea and fresh scent of pines that encroached to within a few hundred yards of the fishing village.

"I daren't go any further like this, Mr. Gate. I know you wanted to get closer to the capitol and all, but the next gale that's coming in looks grey as char and will surely send us to the bottom. And it seems she is a brewing something big up right now. It's coming down from the Ice Sea." He gestured to the mass of dark clouds looming far on the horizon.

"I understand," said Gathelaus. "I trust you will forget you ever saw me and my friend?" He thumbed to his half seasick companion, Niels.

The skipper took his battered hat in one hand and leaned forward. "Honestly, I'm sure those coming after you would just as soon cut my heart out for helping you this far along, so, no, I won't be saying a word."

Gathelaus clapped the skipper on the shoulder and handed him another solid gold piece. Then he and Niels picked up their rucksacks. The sloop eased next to the dock and before she was even tied off the two men had leapt aboard the groaning planks and were striding down the boardwalk taking in the scene.

It was a quaint village with no more than a dozen small huts. There was one church, one stone keep looking as if it were caught frozen in time and ready to tumble to the ground, and one large inn and tavern. There was a stable nearby and from the look of things, despite it being a fishing village, they had good horses.

"They get enough travelers here for an inn that big?" asked Niels.

"It is on the coastal road, but it's not the swiftest way to Hellainik. I'd say we are somewhere on the tip of the peninsula. Out of the way enough that Vikarskeid can't have enough manpower to be sending anyone out here to wait for me."

"You think so? Maybe he has sent out word about a price on your head. One so large he has no intention of ever paying it," suggested Niels.

Gathelaus laughed in agreement, saying, "Likely he has, but who would wait down here? This is the far end of the world and I should know. I've been everywhere."

"You hope."

"Nobody would be waiting here," said Gathelaus.

"There shouldn't have been raiders plying the waters a hundred miles off the coast looking for us either," reminded Niels.

Gathelaus's face darkened. True enough they had been attacked in the middle of the open sea by reavers who recognized the Sellsword King; but that was just bad luck, and hadn't he just sent them to the bottom regardless?

"I need a stout drink," said Gathelaus.

The few folk in the village paid them no mind, seeming more interested in the sloop that had just arrived. A handful of men strode past them to go and see the other new arrivals.

The tavern had a sign out front, hanging from a long rafter by twin chains. It read, *The Wyrm's Tooth*. There was a whitewashed rendition of a long-pointed tooth behind the stylized lettering.

"Odd name for a tavern."

"No, it isn't," said Gathelaus. "Every place like this just wants a story to stand out. What's different is that it isn't a sea related name. You'd think it would be named *Votan's Landing*, or the *Merwife's Chamber*."

They opened the door and went in. A man finished reciting a poem and sat back down amidst a handful of cheers.

"Did you two just get off that ship?" asked an old man.

"Yes," answered Niels.

"Where was she bound from?"

"Mankares," answered Niels with a half-truth.

"Any fruit from the southlands?"

"No."

The old man turned, no longer interested in speaking with them.

Inside the dimly lit tavern, a woman played a melancholy tune on a fiddle that was missing a string. A shaft of light from the damaged roof made all else inside seemed terribly dark by comparison. It was plain that there were a lot of people talking, but they went almost silent, muttering between themselves as the two men walked in.

"Get us a drink, I'll see about buying some of those horses we saw stabled outside," said Gathelaus. Niels nodded and made his way toward the bar. Gathelaus called out, "I have need of horses. I have good coin to pay."

"Here," drawled a mustachioed man at the bar. "I have horses but would need that good coin to part with them. We don't get much travelers down here seeking the few we have."

"I can pay whatever they are worth," said Gathelaus.

"Follow me then," said the man as he got up and went to the door.

Gathelaus looked to Niels and said, "Don't get too comfortable."

Niels shook his head and glanced at his fellow patrons. Most of them wore a simple cloak or tunic. No one had weapons that he could see. He glanced around the room as his eyes became a little more accustomed to the dark. Most of the dozen or so men seated within obviously belonged in an out of the way establishment like this. They were older and looked like fishermen or farmers. There was a barmaid at the far end of the tavern that caught his eye, too. She had an hourglass shape and a heaving bosom. Her dark hair stood out in stark relief from her pale skin.

"I'll have to meet her," he said to himself.

"What can I do you for?" asked the bartender.

Niels acknowledged him then pushed his way to the bar. "I'm famished. I'll also need two ales in the biggest mugs you can find, and I want them served by your prettiest wench!"

"I've only got one, that'd be Dahlia. Hey Dahlia, fetch two ales!" called the barkeep. "She'll help you out."

The pale beautiful woman with black hair and large assets threatening to escape her corset made her way toward him carrying two enormous silver mugs topped with foam-covered ale.

"Thank you kindly, Dahlia," said Niels, attempting his most friendly greeting with his brightest grin. He knew she would have heard everything before, but it didn't hurt to be polite.

"That is two coppers," she said. "Anything to eat is more."

Niels fished the coppers out of his coin purse and slid them across the table to her. She had to lean over a little to retrieve them. He couldn't help but notice the large amber jewel on a golden chain resting between her breasts.

"I am not on the menu," she said softly, without looking at him.

"Of course not, but you can't begrudge me for looking."

"At least you didn't try and toss them down my blouse. Cold coins will not warm my heart for any customer."

Niels smiled. "Well I do try to keep up some hint of gentlemanly manners."

"Anything else?" she asked with a mischievous smile.

"Why is this place called, *The Wyrm's Tooth*?" he asked trying to think of something, anything to keep talking to her.

Dahlia asked, "You really aren't from around here are you?" She pointed behind the bar. High on a mantelpiece and attached to a piece of dark polished wood hung a massive tooth. It must have been as long as a man's hand. It had a slight curve and once Niels looked closely, it seemed that the edge of the tooth had small serrations. There was no doubt that whatever it had belonged to was a magnificent predator.

"That is our claim to fame," she said. "We have one of the only teeth taken from the wyrm."

"A dragon's tooth?"

She looked at him with a smile and nodded proudly.

"So what is that really from?" prodded Niels. "One of those saber-toothed lions I've heard tell of? A tusked man-eating ape perhaps? Or perhaps a great shark?"

Dahlia leaned in. Her brows arched crossly, but he liked the way she moved or at least the way specific parts of her moved.

"It is a wyrm's tooth from the dragon that lives north of here. Have you not heard of the Wyrm of Finnsburg? The killer called Fiendal. All children in the whole of Danelaw know these tales. Who are you stranger?"

FURY \ \ \ JAMES ALDERDICE

Niels was at a loss. Half of his brain was numb from the trip, he was so grateful to be on dry land again, and the other half of his wits was lost in her ample cleavage. "My name?"

"You do have one?" she asked.

"I'm Cap," he stopped himself before saying more.

"Well Cap, you must be new to our lands. Fiendal is the most feared thing in the countryside. Even more so than that pig of a king we have now."

"Who?" he asked dumbly, trying to get his wits about him once more.

"If you don't know, I'm not gonna tell you," she said.

"Tell me about the dragon then," he said. "They don't give their teeth willingly."

She smiled and shook her head. He loved that smile. "They say that a man came riding, born with the fury that burns in all heroes, and he ran a magic sword into the dragon Fiendal and tore free three teeth. That put the dragon to sleep for a hundred years or so, I've been told. But it's awake again now."

"It's awake again?" asked Niels, incredulous. "But that tooth?"

Dahlia smiled. "Uh huh. We have one, another is in Finnsburg Hall and a third went to the king in Hellainik."

"Did he kill the dragon?"

"Of course not. No man can kill a dragon. Anyway, it all happened before I was born," she said. "Wilum, maybe you could recite the tale again?"

FURY ⚔ ⚔ ⚔ JAMES ALDERDICE

"You have a bard here?"

An old man snapped awake and wiped the sleep from his eyes.

"I know it, but I'm not a bard. I'll recite the poem for you, young man, for a copper."

Niels looked to Dahlia who had walked back to the kitchens.

Wilum licked his lips and doffed his cap and held it out to catch the mentioned coin. His white hair stood out erratically now that the cap was not containing it.

Niels was sorry to see Dahlia gone, and with the old man staring at him expectantly, he fished in his coin purse for a copper and tossed it into the old man's cap. "All right, here is a copper for *Not-A-Bard*."

Wilum stood and took a drink from his ale cup, composed himself, leaned slightly on his cane, closed his eyes, and began,

"A king is a man, who rules by his own hand
But t'was heroes like Sigurd Grimsson who tamed this land
Whether blood handed raider, slayer or dark deceiver came
They all met their end with his blade shining red just the same
With bandits, beasts, and buccaneers he did collide
Giving one and all of them that final steel ride
Across the mountains and the plains, his black company rode
And here in the valley, first he heard of that great long tailed toad
For Fiendal the dragon was about and hungered he for blood
The death he wrought on this good land covered it like a flood
Now the sword, spear and axe did brave Sigurd wield

But none of them could break through that dragon skin shield
Steel made by man is what Sigurd intended on Fiendal to feed
Though it was broken bones soon that made the dragon bleed
For no weapon forged by man could strike the deadly blow
It was a blade crafted by a wolf witch don't you know
Halla made a broad double-bladed axe of silver and gold
A wise smith, she covered it with runes ancient and cold
With this weapon in hand alone, did Sigurd knock free
And steal from the dragon teeth numbered but three
Back to his marsh and the cave and back to his lair
Did Fiendal run away and to this day stay there."

Wilum finished, took in a deep breath, and then sat back down. There had been no hesitation nor pause, and Niels had no doubt the old man had memorized the verse long ago. It felt old.

"Very moving," said Niels. "But is any of that true?"

The old man shook his head in disgust. "Didn't I just tell you all about it? The lady just told you about it and you can see the tooth for yourself right there!" Wilum pointed with his cane at the tooth above the mantle.

"Why haven't I heard of this dragon before? This Wyrm of Finnsburg?"

"Because it is like a giant snake you half-wit. They sleep for years once their belly is full. And when they have slept and grown enough, they come out again and the land is cast in misery as they feed an insatiable hunger."

"Let me guess, no one has seen one in a hundred years now?"

Dahlia cocked an eyebrow and looked to Wilum and he back to her.

"Should I tell him then?" asked Wilum.

"Why not?" offered Dahlia. "If he has any sense, if that scares him, he should get back on the boat that brought him here."

"Tell me what?" asked Niels.

Wilum cleared his throat and said, "The stories are all true, after all there is as much truth in myth as there is anything in this world. Maybe more truth than what you hear prattled on as news and wise words in your big cities, ya know-it-all-shite."

"Insults are not an answer," said Niels.

"Answers? It's the truth, I'm telling ya. Fiendal has awakened and is moving over the borderlands, feasting on men and livestock. Makes no never mind to him, I'm sure, whether you believe in him or not. He would eat you just the same."

"Him?"

"Of course, it's a him."

"How do you know that?" asked Niels with a laugh.

Wilum grew flustered and pulled off his cap. His red face stood out in stark contrast to the bushy white sideburns. "Because, he doesn't lay eggs."

"Now there is something. Who has or has not seen a dragon laying eggs that sleeps for centuries?"

"Aye, more wyrm's have been seen deep in the marsh, only Fiendal is greater and thusly sleeps longer than the others."

Niels rocked back on his chair and sipped from his ale. "More monsters, these wyrm's, and they sleep for what, centuries? And now they have awoken, and you know his name and sex. Did I miss anything."

"Don't be rude to the folk who made your drink," said Dahlia.

Niels bowed his head. "I apologize, I'm just trying to understand how much is true and how much is the locals having a go at me."

"That's not an apology," she said.

"I am sorry if I have offended you or the old bard."

"I'm not a bard," said Wilum.

Dahlia stood before him looking cross with her hands on her hips. "I'm not having a go at you. You asked about the legend and we told you. Just be glad you are here and not at Finnsburg Hall."

"I'll make sure I don't go to such a place, lucky for me, my business will take me to Hellainik."

"You're going to the capitol then?" asked Dahlia. "What takes you there?"

"My Lord has urgent business there with the usurper, Vikarskeid."

Niels heard someone move and then go out the door, but he didn't see who it was. He was leery, it could have been trouble, but it also could have been nothing. No one who had been in the tavern looked worthy of his notice when he came in but looks can be deceiving.

"I preferred the Usurper Sellsword to Vikarskeid," said Dahlia. "At least he cared about the kingdom and tried to rule it honorably. But now taxes have gone up and threats from raiders or dragons run rampant without even a hint of protection from the king. We need another revolution."

Her words warmed his heart and where he had just worried about saying too much and the trouble he might be in for speaking his business too loudly, he felt at ease now with Dahlia speaking so plainly in front of the whole tavern.

"I can appreciate your words good, lady, and they do warm my heart. Trust me when I say, change is coming to Vjorn again."

Dahlia laughed.

"What's so funny? I am a fellow patriot of Gathelaus the Usurper King."

She took hold of his shoulder and tugged on his cloak. "I am in a business where I must needs be friends with many creeds and customs, biases and feuds. I told you what you wanted to hear; I saw the blue tartan beneath your cloak. Only a man of Gathelaus would wear that. Vikarskeid has changed the uniform of the army and forbade anyone from wearing the old colors of the guard. If you had a lick of sense you would lose that before any of the king's huntsmen prowling about see you."

"So, you aren't for Gathelaus?" asked Niels, glancing about the room, wondering if he was about to be ambushed.

Dahlia shook her head. "The new king is same as the old king as far as our lives are concerned. It makes little difference to us. But I must be prepared to sing his praises or scorn him with equal enthusiasm depending on the company. Lately there have been men here looking for those such as you."

"How do you know I wouldn't scorn you for saying this?"

She smiled again and touched his cheek. "Your eyes are too kind for me to fear you. I can see the love of life in your eyes. You are a good man."

"You can tell all of that by just looking into my eyes?"

She smiled and nodded. "Of course, I can. A lady in my line of work knows a lot about men. Do you want any supper with that ale? Night will be coming soon."

"Yes, ma'am!"

2. THE DISAGREEMENT

It had been a few minutes and, while Dahlia was preparing his supper Niels sat, just enjoying the moment. It was strange, he had only been talking with her and she had only barely caressed his cheek, but he was more excited by this woman than he had been in anyone for he didn't know how long. His mind raced at the possibilities. Should he remain here? No, he couldn't abandon Gathelaus and the quest to reclaim the crown. He had work to do for his friend, king, and the good of the nation. Perhaps she would ride with them to Hellainik and partake of the revolution to come? No, she was no warrior, she was a barmaid in a tiny fishing village he didn't even know the name of. Perhaps he had simply been away from women too long and was smitten with the first one he had spoken to in weeks. Granted, she was incredibly beautiful.

He almost didn't hear the thunder of rapidly approaching hooves. Guessing it was Gathelaus returning with several horses for their journey, he remained seated, guessing he would have to order another ale for his commander, since he had already downed the one meant for his friend.

But it wasn't Gathelaus entering the tavern. It was a crew of men, perhaps six or seven of them.

Niels was tipsy from the ale and sun coming in behind the men momentarily blinded him.

Once the door was shut and they moved in, he got a better look at them.

Several looked like Tolburnian cutthroats, another one was a big red-haired Azschlander with a massive knife at his belt. Two resembled civilized members of the Sho-Tan horde with conical helmets and long horse sabers, still another seemed to be a slant-eyed killer from Shang-Henj with a long drooping mustache. There was even a small dark Pictish tribesman from the far northern steppes; rumor was that his people ate nothing but meat or whale blubber for they lived along the Ice Sea and had no growing season. A hooded man appeared to be their leader, he entered last and took a place at the far end of the bar with his back to the wall.

Wilum's former surly attitude changed into a bird and flew out the door, he acted like he had somewhere to be and got up to leave the tavern.

"Where are you going, grandfather?" asked the hooded man. "We'll miss your tall tales."

This brought an uproar of laughter from the hooded man's crew, but Wilum was not dissuaded and pushed to get out the door.

One of the conical-helmed men barred his way. "You forgot to ask permission to leave," snarled the man.

"Begging your pardon," said Wilum, almost whimpering. "But can I go please, sir. I'm not feeling well."

All eyes turned to the hooded man to see if he would give his approval.

"Get out," said the hooded man, thumbing toward the door.

Wilum moved as soon as the other shifted his arm out of the way. As he reached the threshold, the man kicked him, sending the old man sprawling into the mud. The crew of cutthroats laughed.

"Is it so hard to get good entertainment?" lamented the hooded man. His men gave a resounding note of black-humored mirth once more.

"Perhaps if you didn't beat them, their tune might sound sweeter," suggested Niels.

The hooded man took notice of Niels and craned his head in wonderment. "Who are you? Music lover?"

"Name is Cap, and that man while he is no bard, didn't deserve that treatment."

The hooded man made a sound that Niels didn't quite understand. Was it a chuckle? A cough? "Cap, huh? You passing through this cursed land?"

"Yep, just passing through."

"Best keep your opinions to yourself then," said the hooded man.

"I always do."

The hooded man grunted and brought a hand to his stubbled chin, which was the only part of his face Niels could see. "Dahlia, a round of mead!" he shouted. "And one for the stranger here, too."

Dahlia brought tankards of mead and gave a slight shake of her head as a warning to Niels to be silent.

"You been traveling far?" asked the hooded man.

"Yes, you wouldn't believe how far," said Niels, as he focused on Dahlia and the large mugs.

"Try me," replied the hooded man.

"Let's just say, I've been places you wouldn't believe."

"I can believe a lot," prodded the hooded man. "Try me."

"Where have you traveled from?" asked Dahlia. "Mankares, right?" She gave another look of *Be Quiet* to Niels.

"A lot farther than that love, a lot farther."

Dahlia rolled her eyes, as if Niels had just said the stupidest thing possible.

"Oh, a world traveler, huh?" taunted the hooded man. "I suppose our backwater here is nothing special to you then. You've seen some fabulous things?"

"I've been lots of places, what's it to you friend?" asked Niels.

The hooded man gave a malevolent chuckle, answering, "I ain't your friend, but I was making polite conversation."

Niels looked the hooded man up and down. He couldn't tell his age or much of anything else about him. The clothing looked well-traveled and worn, but he only had a dagger on his belt and not a sword. Who was he?

Niels replied, "Then it seems we're just having a disagreement. I've traveled far, that's all there is to it."

The hooded man prodded farther. "Maybe all the way from the lost continent, Dar-Al-Hambra and even Hellainik before that, eh?" asked the hooded man pointedly.

"Aw, crap," growled Niels, as the sound of steel sliding from leather filled the room.

The hooded man stood and directed the others. "You're gonna take off that sword belt, without a fuss, or my man behind you will stick that flatbow bolt he has trained on you, right in your skull."

Niels couldn't see the man with the flatbow, but there was no reason to doubt. He could see the fear in Dahlia's eyes as she faced him, and she was looking at someone behind to his left.

Niels remained as calm as he could muster. "Seems you know who I am then?"

"I do, where is the other one?"

"Who?"

"Don't play smart with me. I know a whole lot more than you think. Maybe I just want to know how big a liar you are," threatened the hooded man.

"He went out, looking for horses. Can't say as I know where, since I'm in here with you."

The man grunted and was answered by another man who said, "Truth."

Niels wasn't sure, but he guessed it was the tribal looking savage that had answered.

"How did you know we would come ashore here, of all places, when I didn't know that myself? Our ship was swamped, we should have been a lot farther inland," asked Niels, stalling for time.

"Dagoo here," the hooded man motioned at the Pictish tribesman, "has his ways. He can hardly speak the proper tongue, but he has a way with the spirits. The spirits always know, and if you ask the right questions, they'll tell you."

"Interesting, and who would you be?"

The hooded man said, "I'm Tarbona, and these are my huntsmen. Maybe you've heard of us?"

"Can't say that I have. You been waiting here long?"

"Two days," said Dahlia, sounding annoyed.

"Shut up. And you, hurry and drop that sword belt," ordered Tarbona, as he drew his own sword from beneath his cloak.

"Alight, take it easy," said Niels. He looked at Dahlia again and winked. "Sorry, love." He mouthed silently. *Duck.*

She shook her head, mouthing *Don't.*

Niels reached with his left hand and stole the great crock of ale from her hands while wheeling and drawing his sword with his right. Niels flung the crock back, smashing one of the twisted men in the face and throwing off the aim of the flatbow assassin.

Dahlia screamed and ducked down.

It was a dangerous ploy that worked, the assassin with the flatbow was distracted just enough his timing and aim were thrown. By the fraction of a second he did fire his bolt, Niels had cleaved the conical-helmed man nearest him across the throat and held up the dead man like a shield. This was convenient but unneeded as the wild bolt struck one of the shooters own compatriots in the back, just as he raised a blade against Niels.

The wounded man cried out and went slack with the shock of the bolt.

Niels chopped the wounded huntsman with a shattering blow across the shoulder breaking mail, bone and lungs beneath.

Tarbona raised a sword high for a killing stroke, but Niels kicked a table at him, sending him away, as the sword came smashing down and the flared tip stuck fast in the hardwood.

The regular patrons along with Dahlia and the barkeep fled.

The remaining huntsmen roared and charged with naked blades in their fists. While the tables gave slight room, blocking all the men from crowding him at once, it also made it so Niels could not escape as swiftly as he would have liked. He was fully surrounded by ravenous steel.

Dagoo the Pictish seer slashed with a dagger, but Niels blocked his strike and battered the knife away, he then picked the smaller man up by the scruff of his fetish covered collar and tossed him at the big Azschlander.

"I want his head!" snarled Tarbona.

The front window shattered as a limp body flew inside.

"Boha-Annu's teats!" gasped Tarbona.

It was one of the huntsmen, judging by Tarbona's murderous oath.

The front door burst open, almost knocked off its hinges as Gathelaus shouted, "Out, now!"

Niels made his way toward the door, slashing his sword this way and that.

Gathelaus slammed a spear into the huntsman nearest him, and then another, between he and Niels. The door was cleared, while there were still a host of men roaring for their blood behind. He shut and wedged the spear into the door, holding it shut at least temporarily.

"They'll think twice before leaping out the window," said Gathelaus, with his sword at the ready.

"Now what?" asked Niels.

"We ride out, I have horses."

A flatbow bolt came singing out the broken window and stuck in the post beside Gathelaus's head. It vibrated angry as a kicked hornets' nest.

"Back away. Horses are on the side," urged Gathelaus.

"Did you know they were coming?"

"I had an idea, didn't you?" asked Gathelaus, still watching the broken window. A sword arm reached out flailing blindly and Gathelaus cut off the hand that wielded the blade. A scream from inside, brought a chuckle to his lips.

Niels protested. "You spent the whole time telling me they weren't here!"

Gathelaus led him around the side of the tavern. Four men lay dead on the ground and two fine horses were already saddled and ready to ride. Gathelaus leapt into the saddle. "They had spies listening and watching, we had to make them think they fooled us, the first man that passed us at the docks missed us and thought we were in the boat. But another was inside the tavern."

Niels was incredulous. "You could have said something!"

"I did. I said I'll get the horses!" Gathelaus kicked his horse's flanks and raced away.

Niels followed right behind him as the crowd of bounty hunters broke down the door and staggered from the tavern, cursing. The flatbow man tried another shot but they were already out of range.

As they raced up the hillside, Niels asked, "How many are there?"

"Too many. I killed at least five. You?"

"Four or five. You ever heard of Tarbona?"

"Is that him?"

"That's him, down there in the hood."

"He is supposed to have a tracker that can find anyone. We'll have to kill him, or they'll find us no matter where we go in these mountains."

"We aren't sticking to the coastal road?"

Gathelaus shook his head. "It would take too long and we'd come across more of these huntsmen. Look there." He pointed to the far side of the village where another dozen men were charging after.

Tarbona shouted at them and the mounted men hurried past him in pursuit.

Gathelaus turned his horse about and kicked its flanks. "We need to choose the ground we fight on, until then…"

"Yes?"

"We ride hard and fast to find a good spot for us and a bad spot for them."

"Where would that be?"

"I don't know yet."

They raced down the road, as their pursuers came on, crying for blood.

3. ENCOUNTER IN THE FOREST

They had only a small lead on their pursuers and Gathelaus knew the horses would soon tire. The one benefit he could think was that his horses were rested, while those of the men behind them had been run coming to the village. It wasn't a lot, but it was something for the sake of whose mounts would run out first.

He knew enough of horses to have selected the best ones the coastal man had to offer. But there were at least twenty men coming after them, several of them armed with flatbows. Hard to cut down that many men no matter how good you are with a sword if you're getting pin-cushioned with bolts designed to punch through mail.

He glanced over his shoulder. They were still coming.

At a fork in the road, Niels shouted, "Which way? Should we split up?"

"No, that wouldn't help anything, there are too many," said Gathelaus.

"Which way then?"

"Can you read the waybills?"

Their horses thundered closer to the signpost. A tall man stood beside the crossroads, a lute over his shoulder. He raised a hand in greeting.

"Is that one of the huntsmen?" asked Niels.

"Looks like just a bard."

Niels peered closer at the signpost. "Danelaw to the left, Finnsburg to the right."

Gathelaus looked back. The pursuers were less than a half-mile behind them. There was not enough cover to fool them on their course yet, nor were the trees along the road in a position where he could try an ambush. "We ride toward Finnsburg, it's on the road to Hellainik."

Niels nodded and hurried to the right.

As they raced past, Gathelaus noticed that someone had scrawled a skull and crossbones over the signpost pointing toward Finnsburg. It was also not lost on him that there were no new tracks going that direction. But with their pursuers already too close, he gave it no more thought.

The tall man standing beside the crossroads looked at them with a jovial mustached face, shouting, "Oh, you're going by so fast, stop and I'll sing the ballad of Molly with the Seven Nipples."

"No time friend," answered Niels as they raced past.

"Next time then," answered the bard giving them a friendly salute.

Grey clouds roiled overhead as the storm moved in at an incredible gallop. A touch of rain began to fall, just enough to splash them in the face with cold.

The road had deep ruts from old wagon tracks but was not muddy yet. It soon could become a bog. The grass along the edges was brittle and yellow and would easily betray their tracks if they should try an overland course to elude their foes. The trees were not thick either and would not hide them from a keen-eyed man.

Niels asked, "Do you see a good place to make a stand yet?"

"None of this is ideal yet, too flat, no cover, we could easily be surrounded and shot through by flatbows."

"My horse is tiring," gasped Niels, as he looked back at the huntsmen who were still on their track but falling slightly farther behind.

"Mine too," said Gathelaus. "We might not have a choice soon enough. But we have gained a quarter mile on them."

They hurried on and the rain hurried on to become sleet. Grey ice coated the ground and Gathelaus watched for anywhere he might be able to leave the road and yet still hide their passage.

The road curved and they found a spot where a small brown creek, swollen from the rains, overstepped its banks. It was about as wide as the road and yet still shallow, for they could see boulders and such cutting the surface.

"This may be as good as it gets. We ford here and try to find a place to cross leaving them guessing. With any luck the storm will cover our tracks and buy us more time."

"It's coming down hard, maybe we have already lost them," said Niels hopefully.

Gathelaus shook his head. "Not with that Pictish tracker and shaman. If anything, we have just bought a day."

FURY ✧ ✧ ✧ JAMES ALDERDICE

They left the road and waded into the brown creek. The horses were skittish, disliking the cold murk that they could not see the bottom of. They hurried downstream more than a quarter mile, always watching their back trail to be sure they were not seen.

"I can't see the bottom. What if the horse breaks a leg?"

"Worth the risk, we gotta lose them. The murk will hide our trail, too." They trotted their horses downstream. The sleet turned into snow, swirling about in nasty gusts.

Niels said, "This cold might do us in, if they don't get us first."

Gathelaus snorted in reply, but he watched their back trail with worry. "This is about as far as I dare, they may hit the stream soon enough."

"Let's take the chance and go past that bend in the hills," said Niels.

Gathelaus watched behind them. "All right but hurry, speed that horse up."

They trotted down the stream toward a cut in the banks where the water had made a channel through some low-slung hills. After they passed beyond, Gathelaus waited at a spot where he could only just see the road. It was getting difficult, because of the building snow caught in the wind.

"We've lost them for now, but we best get out of the stream and find some shelter."

"These banks are steep, if we climb out here, they'll see our tracks, snow or not."

Gathelaus gritted his teeth. "All right, we ride down a little farther."

They followed the stream as it meandered back and forth. The banks remained steep and the trees closed in. The snow thankfully eased a slight amount.

A small wolf, perhaps only a yearling, watched them from a bank. They heard a yip and then, just a little farther down, they saw two more. Neither of these were large either.

"Should we be concerned?" asked Niels. "Where is their mother?"

"I don't think a pack would be interested in two armed men, but their curiosity is something. They should run off at the sight of a man."

They heard a large splash in the water not far in front of them.

"What was that?" asked Niels.

"Don't know. Keep your eyes on the left, I'll watch the right, but trust your horse's instincts."

The trees grew thicker and, while they could see the creek flowing on in front of them, between the branches and the light skiff of snow, they could not see far ahead.

Something brown jerked in the water ahead of them. It thrashed once more before going still.

"Did I tell you about the dragon I heard tell roams these borderlands?" said Niels.

"Be silent," growled Gathelaus as he unsheathed his sword. Niels followed suit.

As the overhanging branches thinned and they came around the edge of the serpentine course in the creek, they saw the hind end of a deer lying sideways in the water. Its head was under the water, its mighty rack stuck out.

Atop the stag crouched the largest wolf they had ever seen. With a single paw, it held down the deer whose wounds turned the brown waters red. It growled at them and then, astonishingly, it stood up on two legs.

Its hands were human like, though covered with grey fur and each long fingertip ending in black talons. It had a massive muscular build, large enough to rival a titan. It stood as tall as they did upon horseback.

They were at a standstill. Neither wishing to intrude any further toward the beast nor turn their back upon it. The horses could hardly contain their fear and it was all each man could do to keep their mounts from panicking and running off.

The yellow-eyed monster stared at them, its white teeth gleaming between the spaces where red painted them.

Finally, Gathelaus said, "Go your way beast and allow us to go ours, we shall not trouble your woods but leave in peace."

It picked up the deer carcass with one mighty hand and said in a voice that was kin to the thunder, "Come not again to my wood."

"You have my word," answered Gathelaus.

"What is your name?" it asked in a deep rasp, as if questioning his vow.

"I am Gathelaus Thorgrimson."

"Thorgrim? I knew a Thorgrim once many years ago."

That struck Gathelaus as exceedingly odd. His father had never spoken of an encounter with a creature such as this, but there were many things his father had never told him.

"I grant you safe passage. Leave my wood," it commanded, pointing a taloned finger to their left.

"My thanks," Gathelaus paused, wondering if he should ask the creature its name, but he decided better. "Men may come hunting for me. Huntsmen serving a tyrant. My apologies if they disturb you."

The wolfshead beast squinted its eyes but answered firmly, "Foes of a son of Thorgrim, are my foes as well."

"My thanks," was all Gathelaus could manage.

The wolfman leapt up the side of the steep embankment, still clutching the stag with that hideous strength, and disappeared into the woods to their right.

Niels looked to Gathelaus, speechless.

"We go to the left and away from these woods."

Niels nodded vigorously.

They carefully made their way up the left bank, heedless of how much it dug into the reddish earth, and up into the woods. Niels made his way through the thick trees while Gathelaus paused a moment to look back. He could sense better than see the gleaming yellow eyes that watched them from afar. He saluted the monster's memory and rode after his friend.

4. ROLL THE BONES

They were tired, wet, and hungry, but Gathelaus insisted they give more space to the wolfish monster. "We can't expect a truce we don't honor," he said, as much to himself as Niels.

"But the horses," said Niels. "I think they are on the verge of faltering."

"So we walk," agreed Gathelaus.

They dismounted and trudged over the brambles and fallen logs in the woods. It was perilously slow going and each man couldn't help but watch behind them as nervously now as they had when pursued by Tarbona's huntsmen.

The snow fell again in blinding sheets and all sunlight had fled the land.

Niels said, "We must find shelter. Do you think we have given the monster enough room?"

"It will have to do. If we don't give them a rest they will fall dead," said Gathelaus.

They found a thick copse of trees, and while Niels started a small fire, Gathelaus built a windbreak with logs and then covered that over with green branches.

It was difficult to get the fire going as the wind cruelly insisted on blowing it out. Not until Gathelaus's windbreak was finished, did the coals catch. Even then the work was not done, as they brushed down their mounts and gave them grain that Gathelaus had purchased beforehand.

They took off their boots and tried to dry their clothing as best they could, but the slanting fall of the snow fell among them and clung to their cloaks and froze their mail.

Darkness was lifted slightly by a bright moon that stole above the heavy clouds, but the snow never completely stopped. They took turns being on watch and feeding the fire throughout the night to keep some warmth close to their bodies.

Without a word being said, each felt they were being watched—likely by the beast for huntsmen in the wet woods would not have been so patient.

When at last daybreak teased upon the horizon, the snow ceased. Sunlight danced out from behind the morning clouds and warmed their skin.

They were still exhausted but alive. The rest had the done the horses much good and by the time they broke camp, the sun was melting the snow every place but where the shadows fell.

Finding a road before midday, they trotted along at a good pace, still wary to be away from the woods of the monster as well as the likely pursuit of the huntsmen. The feeling of being watched never fully left, but once the trees thinned, it seemed less worrisome.

As they rode on, the trees grew sparser and they came to an upland where reddish cap rock made majestic spires among jutting canyons and valleys.

Gathelaus said, "I'm not sure we are even on the same road we were at the crossroads the first time. That wood was thick and treacherous and for all we know, we took a magnificent shortcut, but I can tell we are still heading in the correct northeasterly direction to reach a main thoroughfare and take us back to Hellainik."

"At least we are well away from that monstrous wolfhead's wood," said Niels.

"Aye, it would be unfortunate if we ever had a need to go back there and face the thing. But I had heard no tales of it preying upon folk in the countryside, especially so near the coast and that fishing village."

"I don't even know the name of that place, but I wish I did."

"Why?"

Niels laughed. "I think I'm in love with the bar maid, Dahlia."

"You've been away a long time, that can happen."

Niels rode closer, saying, "We can't all be as cavalier about women as you. I've hardly heard a word about Coco from you in days, nor have you spoken of Nicene in some time."

"Nicene is dead. Won't do me any good dwelling on her. Life is for the living not the dead."

Niels countered, "You don't need to be this stony with me. I knew and cared for her, too."

Gathelaus ignored the opening saying, "And Coco is crafty, perhaps she has been able to escape Hawkwood's clutches."

"Crafty as she may be, Hawkwood is more so."

Gathelaus nodded. "If she lives, she will be my queen. But sometimes I think I am cursed to always have those I care about stolen from me."

"You once said that was simply the gamble we must face in life."

"True enough. Look a crossroads."

Before them was a towering mesa and the road forked each way around. It was impossible to say if it merged once more beyond or not. Each path continued a somewhat north easterly direction just at varied angles.

"Where are we?" asked Niels.

"The borderlands between Danelaw, the capitol kingdoms, and another lesser kingdom."

"Finnsburg?"

"That's it. Their lord Hoskuld was loyal to me and sent men for the levies after the fall of Forlock."

Niels answered, "Rumors in the tavern. They say a dragon has returned and is a pox upon Finnsburg."

"A dragon? Here?"

"So they said. I heard his name is Fiendal and that he was returning after a long sleep."

Gathelaus searched his memory. "I'm sure that most of the men levied from Finnsburg were slain by that sorcerer Vikarskeid set upon me. He must have crushed more than fifty men and horses all wearing the armor I bid them to wear. Can't imagine my name will be a very popular one in Finnsburg. I've nothing to show for their dead and my usurper sits upon the throne. They can't be very popular with Vikarskeid either. And now they are cursed with a dragon?"

"That's why that tavern was called the Wyrm's Tooth. They supposedly had one of three teeth that had been knocked out of its mouth by an ancient hero over the mantle there."

Gathelaus pondered. "Yes, I heard stories in my youth, but didn't think they could be true, but there is more truth in myth, than in…"

Niels cut him off. "I heard the same from an old man in the tavern."

"It is an old saying."

"Do you think there could be dragons once more? I had heard they were all gone, but there was the one in KhoPeshli."

Gathelaus shifted uncomfortably at the memory. "But that was a sorcerer possessing a dragon's body."

"It wasn't a necrotic dragon; it had wings and blew fire and everything."

"True enough, it must have come from somewhere, and Ole did say something about dragons being awakened down upon some holy mountain far south of Valchiki. Perhaps that event woke more than just the one we saw before? Maybe it woke them wherever they slept all over the world?"

"The bard in the tavern said that sometimes the wyrms can sleep for ages. Sounds like this one has awakened, and now it's hungry after a good long sleep of centuries."

Gathelaus considered that. "Could be. And that was near Finnsburg?"

"So they said."

"Then I hope that was on another path, we have enough troubles of our own to attend to without fighting another lost cause."

Niels laughed, despite himself. "You were the one to personally take care of the warring wizards in Aldreth, slay the basilisk, defeat the demon of the Silent Island, throw down the anti-gods of Tultecacan, and destroy the Pipe of Mahmackrah; and now you wish to avoid this mere dragon Fiendal?"

Gathelaus grimaced. He had no wish to meet a dragon again, the other had been difficult enough to kill, and he had needed sorcery and his companion of old, Ole, to do it. "If the gods set that path before me, then I will do what heroes do."

"And that is?" prodded Niels.

Gathelaus breathed heavily. "The hero does the right thing regardless of it being a lost cause. I will slay a dragon, if we find ourselves on that road."

"We are at a crossroads. Which way?"

"I don't know. Roll the bones to decide."

Niels reached into his belt and withdrew a large die. "Better than ten, we go left." He tossed it in the air and caught it. He frowned.

"What is it?"

"One. We go right."

"Bad luck. You should have let it hit the ground."

"And get off my horse?"

Gathelaus shrugged.

Niels frowned at him but dismounted and threw the die in the air. It hit the ground and tumbled, rolling over itself numerous times before coming to a stop on one once again.

"Damnit. I should throw this one away."

Gathelaus laughed, saying, "Do what you like, but it won't change that you rolled it twice. Seems we are meant to go to the right once more."

"All right but the next time, if there is a choice, we take the left-hand path."

Gathelaus laughed again. "Whatever you think is easier."

"Whatever, I think? You give the illusion of choice."

They rode on in silence for some time, going further into the cap rock tablelands. Here and there spots of dark red rock would stand up amidst towering buttes. Trees dotted the land thicker where water might pool at the base of canyons, though few grew to any real height.

Niels lamented, "Crossroads are rumored to be evil places."

Gathelaus shrugged in the saddle. "Most cities are built upon crossroads."

"What did I say," said Niels with a laugh. "Evil places."

Grey clouds formed above them and even with the early afternoon's light, the sky grew darker.

Niels said, "Once we get back, I have an idea where YonGee and our other confederates may be hiding, but it will take time to marshal your forces and bring the revolution to Vikarskeid."

"I wonder that I shouldn't just come upon him like a thief in the night and slay him and throw his corpse to the dogs," growled Gathelaus.

"He has many men who side with the old class of nobles. He has hired many mercenaries and such like Tarbona to watch for you. Not to mention Hawkwood."

Gathelaus nodded as he ran a hand over his stubbled chin. "Perhaps, but his gold must run out sometime. He cannot tax his way to covering his own ass forever."

"He would certainly try."

Gathelaus laughed.

The rain fell again in driving sheets and the road was turned into a muddy track. Lightning clapped overhead and Gathelaus wondered if the gods were smacking their own tankards together at the great sound.

"We should find shelter again," suggested Niels.

"Aye, but there are few enough safe places in a landscape like this. We must avoid the canyons where flashfloods could come flowing through, and even caves here could fill if they are in the wrong shelter."

"Then, where?"

"I see a light on those far hills, could be a village or fortress."

"That's at least ten miles."

"There is nowhere else to go in this rain," lamented Gathelaus.

"Just once I would like to stay in a tavern with a pretty lady and not have to rush out the door."

Gathelaus leaned over in the saddle and slapped him on the back. "I saw her, too; we'll go back someday."

They rode on through the hard-falling rain, the trees whipping and waving.

Niels leaned in the saddle closer so that he might whisper to Gathelaus, "Just behind us and to my right, I thought I saw the wolfshead watching."

Gathelaus turned and looked but saw nothing. "Your instincts are probably right. But he sees we are moving and not lingering to cause harm in his wood, if he still considers this his domain. I don't believe he shall cause us trouble."

"I hope you're right."

"Monstrous as he may be, I did not get the feeling of evil from him," answered Gathelaus with a shrug.

"Hard to believe that thing wouldn't be a danger."

Gathelaus chuckled, "I didn't say it wasn't dangerous, just not evil. Course if I'm wrong, keep your blades high and sharp."

5. THE NIGHT STALKER

As twilight approached the rain ceased, but a thick mist rose off the marsh and the road was soon hidden beyond a score of paces ahead of themselves. They crossed by numerous pools of water surrounded by cattails and small trees.

"There is something off the side of the road ahead," said Niels.

"Keep your blades ready," cautioned Gathelaus. He watched the trees on either side of the road for any hint of movement and watched his horse too to see if it should smell or hear something beyond his own senses. The horse snorted and stamped its foot, but he could smell a putrid odor, too, that did not denote an ambush, at least not one for himself.

A wagon lay on its side, pushed to the side of the road.

"A tinker's wagon. Looks like it is still full of his wares," said Niels as he rode around the backside of it.

"I don't think this is a trap for us," said Gathelaus, though he remained mounted and watched all about them. Somewhere far off a raven cried warning.

"The cargo has been rifled through, but I still see silver and copper accruements here. Here is a box of knives and a fine stewpot. This was not a robbery."

"What then?" teased Gathelaus, letting Niels answer his own questions.

FURY ⸸ ⸸ ⸸ JAMES ALDERDICE

"Even if the wagon wrecked and overturned in the mud, a good driver could have re-hitched his team and pulled it back up. And who would leave all their goods and livelihood lying beside the road for anyone passing by to claim? Why has no one taken it?"

"Why?" goaded Gathelaus.

"Where is the tinker and his team?"

"I think I found him." Gathelaus pointed not more than a dozen paces away.

Niels strode to where Gathelaus directed.

In a pile, mixed with wretched offal and hooves, was a leering broken skull and unhinged jaw.

"What the devil!" shouted Niels, holding his mouth over his nose.

Gathelaus now held his hand over his nose and mouth, too. His horse stamped, anxious to be away from this place.

"What could do such a thing?"

"What indeed but a dragon that could swallow a man's head whole, digest and excrete it?"

"Along with the hooves from his team?" marveled Niels.

Gathelaus glanced over the area. "His team lies over there. I see the oxen's head and horns. Too wide for the monster, so he spit them out. Judging the pile, I'd say this occurred no more than three days ago."

"That recent?"

Gathelaus grimly nodded.

"Let us be away from this place and hurrying on to where we saw those lights, for shelter."

"Aye, I think the rain will return soon," said Gathelaus, as he urged his all too eager horse forward.

They trotted on at a good clip, keeping a wary eye out among the marsh and trees. Ravens circled in the twilight not far ahead and Gathelaus couldn't help but wonder if they waited beside another victim of the dragon's wrath, or perhaps beside the monster, waiting for their own leftover scraps. But as the rain began again, as well as the encroaching darkness, the carrion birds went and roosted farther away into the woods.

"I can't see that light anymore," said Niels.

"Nor I, but it was a few miles farther ahead on this road, I am sure."

They trotted on, none too fast as the mud went deep for the flowing rain and they didn't wish to race their horses into a bog for fear of the twisting serpentine path in the gathering gloom.

Thunder rolled over the land and slammed heavily. Crashing arcs of lightning illuminated weird swaths of the grotesque landscape and strange things swirled in the pooled waters at their elbows.

"I like not this place nor the storm," said Niels. "Let us hurry on and find that shelter we saw earlier."

Gathelaus grimly nodded and they hurried their tired mounts along the muddy track.

FURY ⚔ ⚔ ⚔ JAMES ALDERDICE

Thunder boomed again, but this time, though it was farther away, they felt its power nearer, penetrating the ground beneath their feet as if it had been pounded like a kettle drum.

"Something is out there," said Niels. "The wolf?"

Gathelaus shook his head. "Arm yourself but let us make haste."

They rode on at a greater pace and the ground rocked underfoot as if the beating of their hearts was matched by earth itself. The fog curled and lifted in the storm winds only to dive again and slither over them.

The terrible sound of a momentous growl came from the mist ahead and blackness revealed nothing but the continued tramp of doom drawing near.

Their horses reared in terror and Niels was thrown to the mud. Gathelaus hardly managed control of his own as it stamped and panicked, nearly trampling the fallen Niels.

"Get up!" cried Gathelaus.

Niels moaned and rolled over to his hands and knees as he found his breath. Splattered and covered with mud, he laughed. "I almost thought that thunder was something else."

"It was," said Gathelaus, giving him a hand and swinging his friend up on the saddle behind himself.

Not far ahead of them on the road, they heard Niels's horse scream in horror as a terrible roar rocked the night. The snapping of bones and great slabs of torn flesh slapped wet in the night. An invisible gullet was jammed with meat and they heard gluttonous swallowing not more than a hundred paces in the darkness from themselves.

The foul scent of opened bowels and blood maddened Gathelaus's horse. Rearing in a crazed panic, the horse threw Gathelaus, he landed in the mud beside Niels who was thrown a second time.

Hulking steps lunged after the direction of the fleeing horse in the dark, and the mist concealed great feet that trod upright, bipedal, walking at a hideous pace, beating like the slave drum on a pirate galley.

They each heard the thing pass by them less than a dozen strides away. The mist and darkness so thick it concealed the thing and they saw only a great black shadow race by, tall as a house.

The steady beat of its feet, slamming in pursuit of the mad horse. It roared again, and the horse screamed in terror and agony.

"That must have been twelve feet tall," said Niels.

"Not a wolf."

"That ran on two legs," said Niels.

"Lets us do the same, at least until we must face it," suggested Gathelaus.

They ran as fast as they could in the opposite direction, slipping and sliding in the mud.

A short time later they came across the carcass of Niels's horse, or at least what was left of it. Some of the head and rear legs sprawled on the ground. The saddle and saddle bags had fallen a short way away, but the ribs, forelegs and guts were gone. The thick copper smell of blood wafted from across the road.

"I never saw the like," murmured Niels, as he took up the saddle bags.

"That reminds me," said Gathelaus. "Everything I own but what I'm wearing was on that horse."

"Better to be alive, let's go," urged Niels.

Gathelaus agreed and they hurried on down the misty path.

Far away they heard the shadowy monster roar, and the snapping of bones echoed over the moor.

They hurried as fast as their bruised legs could carry them, slipping and sliding in the mud on the ribbon of road.

The sliver of moon came from behind the clouds and they saw ahead of them a glade with a farmhouse crouched on a slight uplift.

"Shelter?"

Gathelaus shrugged. "Perhaps. I don't see a light anywhere. It might not be the light we saw earlier."

"Looks deserted. But shelter is shelter."

They hurried on, reaching the farmstead as cold beams of moonlight washed over the stucco surface. It was a simple affair, thatch roof and small windows set in thick walls. The door was smashed off its hinges and a good portion of the threshold destroyed. They couldn't help but imagine that the monster had broken inside and devoured any who were unfortunate enough to remain.

Niels glanced at the door and the snapped bar that should have held it firm. "It's like a battering ram hit this. That plank should have withstood any roadside bandit. This monster's strength is incredible."

"You said it was a dragon," reminded Gathelaus.

"Dragons don't walk on two feet, do they? They crawl on four and have wings and breathe fire."

"Does it matter?"

Examining the broken threshold and scanty living area that had been rooted through as if hogs had found it, Niels agreed, "I suppose not. It looks like whatever it is reached in and tore everything apart. There is no one here."

"Judging by the horses, it would have swallowed man, woman, and child whole without a problem."

As if in answer to their query, the terrible roar of the beast echoed through the night, its tramping steps heading in their direction.

"What now?"

"We make a stand, what else is there to do?"

The footsteps of doom drew nearer.

6. THE RABBITS DEN

The terrible throbbing beat of the approaching gait drew ever closer. Gathelaus guessed with the clearing of the mist in the glade before the broken homestead, he would see the monster when it was within two dozen paces. Still far too close for comfort, but he was tired of running, and there was nothing left to do but face the fear.

"Over here, you fools!" urged an emphatic voice.

A man peeked at them from beneath a large oaken hatch.

They hurried to his hiding place where they saw him standing fully erect down in the ground, holding a lantern.

"Speak quickly, who are you? Why should I let you in to my retreat?"

"I am Gate, this is Niels. We are Blade Wardens."

"Fools!" he spat at them. "We have dealt with Fiendal now two moons and the king finally sends two imbeciles to die on their first day."

"It's night," said Niels.

The thundering tramp of the dragon drew nearer. The steady tramp of its two legs beat in primal rhythm.

"I should leave you to die, but I won't. Climb in. Hurry now, I can't have the monster smelling us out."

The man moved back from the hatch and Niels and Gathelaus dropped inside. The man hurriedly picked up a bucket of some foul-smelling substance and splashed it outside the hatch, then shut it tight and barred it closed with a stout plank.

The hole, which Gathelaus guessed to be a root cellar, smelled as foul as any war campaign hospital he had ever been to. The sour scent of sulphur permeated the space.

"The stink is on account of living like this, but the sulphur also dissuades the dragon," explained the man.

There was a small pile of potatoes and other food items stored at the far end of the wall. A woman and two small children also huddled inside.

"I'll thank you not to bother my wife and little ones. They've been through enough," said the man.

"Who are you?" asked Gathelaus.

The man sniffed. "I'm Knut Hrakkison. I farm the southern fields of Hoskuld. Or I did."

"The dragon?" asked Niels, pointing back at the hatch.

"Silence now!" urged Knut.

The heavy tread of the dragon approached. The mother held a hand over each of the children's mouths as she shut her eyes. Tears welled there and ran across her cheeks, so terrible was her fear.

A strong snort blasted air just outside the hatch, sending dust flying away from the sill. A force pressed against the oaken slab, and then a long, shearing scrape sounded as Fiendal surely ran a talon over the wood. The hatch flexed with the pressure, but it did not give.

It snorted once more, then they heard the familiar thump of its stride as it left the farmstead.

Only after the monster had been gone several minutes did Knut speak. "This is how we must live every night now to survive. We leave our home and shelter here. Every day I farm what I can, but it is hard work, I have lost all livestock. I have no help."

"Your home?" asked Gathelaus.

Knut continued, "I repaired my door the first couple times, but Fiendal breaks it down every time he comes by. He even did the one time I left the door wide open, as if it was an affront to him. He is no stupid beast. He is proud and vindictive, but not stupid."

"Is all of the countryside like this?"

Knut nodded. "Those that live have had to adapt. We live like frightened rabbits. Doing what work we can in the day and living in holes in the night when the monster chooses to roam."

"How long has this been going on?" asked Gathelaus.

"Ain't you King Vikarskeid's Blade Wardens sent to do something about it?"

"How long?" demanded Gathelaus.

"Three months," answered Knut, seeming confused by the question.

"And no one has done anything about the dragon?"

Knut snorted. "What can any man do against a dragon? You two must have been on somebody's shit list to be sent here. His skin is like iron, nothing can cut it. There is no puncturing his outside. His teeth are like swords, and his feet are worse, claws as big as a steer's horns. He kills with his feet or his mouth."

"No fire?" asked Niels.

"Fire?" asked Knut confusedly. "No, I haven't tried fire, but I'd never get close enough to attempt that neither."

"No, I mean does it breathe fire?"

"Fire? No, it's not a damn wizard."

Gathelaus asked, "Does Lord Hoskuld still live?"

"So far as I know. Didn't he send for you? Are you Blade Wardens of the king or not?"

"I don't serve Vikarskeid," said Gathelaus, finally.

Knut held up a pitchfork. "Well who are you then? Bandits? Think you can come in and rob the countryside because it is destroyed now, huh? Well, more the pity on you, there's no wealth here. Look at my stores there, potatoes, beets, and onions, and when that's gone, we'll die. We won't make it through the winter like this. There are hardly no livestock left to the land and most folk are dead. So try me if you must, but I'll bleed you before I go down."

"Hold," said Gathelaus. "I'd never do harm to you or your family."

"Family," sniffed Knut. "I lost my eldest son to Gathelaus the Usurper when he asked for a levy of men, then my other two boys and a daughter were taken by Fiendal. My family is almost gone."

Gathelaus watched the mother clutch the two young children close, tears rained from her eyes.

"I will find a way to end this scourge," he said. "I swear it."

Knut shook his head. "Like I said, you are a pair of fools."

"Maybe, but I am Gathelaus, the Usurper King."

"I was wrong," said Knut. "You're a wandering mad man."

"No, he speaks the truth," said his wife. "I saw him once in Hellainik. Not so covered with mud, or with the beginnings of a beard growing, but it is him."

Knut cast a wary eye over Gathelaus, then cried out and raised his pitchfork menacingly once again.

Gathelaus made no move to defend himself.

"Husband, no!" cried his wife.

Knut glanced over his shoulder at her, then slammed the pitchfork into the shelving beside Gathelaus and dropped to his knees, growling in despair.

Gathelaus put a hand on Knut's shoulder, saying, "I owe your family for its support more than I can repay, but I will cleanse this foul creature from the land or die trying."

"Nothing can be done," said Knut through falling tears.

"Tell me all you can of the dragon," said Gathelaus.

Knut began, "Once Finnsburg was a place of joy and happiness. It was ideal farming country, wide long meadows fenced in by marshes stocked with fish, stout pine forests and snow-clad mountains. Situated halfway between the Danelaw and Hellainik roads, Lord Hoskuld's family sold cattle and grain in all directions."

"At least he did, until the dragon, called Fiendal awoke.

"The wise women foretold of a good harvest and there was. When Sow-Wein, the final harvest festival, was nigh, the people in the hamlet of Finnsburg gathered to find joy. We came together and danced and sang. The great golden Hall of Lord Hoskuld was finished and blessed that it would be our hamlet's crowning jewel.

"Lord Hoskuld declared a celebration. He gave each man a gold and silver ring, a generous bonus for our labors. He brought in a grand piano and a dozen bards for the harvest festival night. Barrels of beer and casks of whiskey were divvied out freely, and even the red-lantern girls from Hellainik came. They all banged the drum and sang the songs of life, lust, and laughter. And we reveled as loudly throughout the valley as had never been heard since the dawn of time when Fiendal himself was spawned.

"So rudely awoken from his long slumber, the stalking demon despised the raucous melodies and blaring horns, the giggling women and carousing men. Waiting until dark, the monster watched, and when even the horned moon hid behind a veil of clouds, he struck—for his heart was both vicious and cruel. He delighted in the fear and drank deeply of our terror.

"Tramping into the carnival square with the speed of a ravening wolf, Fiendal slashed both man and beast. Horses screamed as they were torn apart and men cried out for their mothers as they died. The lizard's mighty jaws clamped down, and those that could ran and hid in deep shadows. He crushed oxen and armored footmen and swallowed drunken snoring fools slumbering upon card tables.

Some brave souls tried to slay the demon, but nothing could penetrate his thick scaly hide. The thunderous repeat of sword strokes, curses, and arrows, and spikes only further upset the monster and these men only died next.

"Fiendal slew thirty souls, and by dawn's early light the nightmare vanished back into the misty marsh. His great three-toed tracks left a wake of such awful destruction upon Finnsburg Hall that men whispered afterward across the territories when mentioning the doomed hamlet, for fear that they may summon the dread demon to their own abode.

"Heroes and hunters came, mighty men all, and yet these mighty heroes and hunters died as no bolt or blade could harm the thick-scaled monster. Too wise for poison or traps, immune to spells and wards, Fiendal has become a blight on a once fair land. Shamans and wizards from the five nations were consulted and all said the same, this land was Fiendal's. Leave it to him or die.

"Hoskuld is a stiff-necked man and he refused to leave his family's land and he remained there with a handful of folk, though he hid behind thick doors in small rooms when the sun went down.

"In the weeks that followed, the monster returned chaotically, feeding upon whatever it found whether man or beast. Finnsburg soon had more ghosts than men to work the land and it is said bad luck covers the house of Hoskuld like flies over stink." Knut finished and sat back on his haunches.

Knut's wife, however, took up the last, saying, "Lord Hoskuld's golden hall of dreams and lands have been a sad and somber place full of grim despair, and will remain so, until a king comes riding."

7. SOUR WELCOMES

The next morning, when Knut assured them it was safe to travel short distances as Fiendal seemed to only hunt after sundown, they began the walk to Finnsburg.

Knut walked them to the road and pointed the way, saying, "They won't likely have any horses for you, they've probably all been devoured, but you could always ask. In these parts, an animal is probably worth more than any five in your cities, but everyone is afraid it won't last once Fiendal breaks in and steals them dead."

"I'm grateful for your taking us in," said Gathelaus.

"Our pleasure," said Knut's wife.

Knut grimaced.

Gathelaus said, "Did you know about a tinker's wagon, a mile back down the road? He won't be coming back for any of it. He's dead."

Knut shook his head. "No, might have some good things I suppose, but I've been struggling to just have food for my family. Winter will be mighty harsh without a supper."

Gathelaus said, "You should at least grab some things from the tinker's wagon for yourself, then. Our thanks for your hospitality for the night."

Knut shook his head. "I've lost my faith in many ways, but I hope you can do something against this monster."

"A king can find a way with the gods help," said his wife, as they bid he and Niels goodbye.

Rain fell like tears as Gathelaus and Niels approached Finnsburg. It was seated on a low hill overlooking the valley. It was as commanding a view as could be afforded here. There was a low stone wall, no more than eight feet, topped with wooden pikes another four feet high that surrounded several acres around the homes and hall. The great hall was the main feature amidst the thatch covered homes and barn. It was as large as any hall Gathelaus had seen at numerous castles and kingdoms, standing perhaps three to four stories high, but there was not even a wisp of smoke rising from its many chimneys.

As they approached, they saw no clear sign of habitation and wondered momentarily if perhaps it was truly deserted. Knut said he had not visited its walls, despite the proximity, for many days.

They strode through the broken gates and were surprised to be challenged by a scrawny buck-toothed wall warden. "Who're you?" demanded the wall warden with fear only slightly hidden by disdain. "We have no truck with beggars here, be gone!"

Gathelaus ignored him and walked on into the empty courtyard. It was strewn with refuse and stunk of death. "Where is your lord?" he asked, knowing his voice burned like hot hammered iron.

The wall warden leveled his spear unsteadily, "I said be off with you! Before I call a dozen men to come slay you both!" He held out a horn as if he might summon an army.

Gathelaus gave a disarming smile, knowing it did not conceal his penetrating gaze. Armed as they were, they should have been perceived as fighting men, but covered in mud and blood, the wall warden foolishly assumed them to be beggars come calling in a starving kingdom.

Niels snatched the spear from the wall warden's hand, saying, "Call your fifty men, or can you conjure fifty corpses by the smell of the place?"

The wall warden looked about disarmed as he was, but neither stranger made a further move at him.

"I'll have you for that," he protested at Niels for taking his spear.

"Where is your lord?" asked Gathelaus again. "Take me to him."

He gripped the wall warden's arm like a bear trap, twisting it hard and firm as if to break his bones. "Name's Gathelaus. I'm here to see Hoskuld," he answered, the slack-jawed watchman.

"You're Gathelaus? Was the king? Sorry, I reckon. Follow me then."

"Uh huh." Gathelaus followed the wall warden to the manor house.

The wall warden said, "The yellow-haired man at the door is Bors, my commander. Lord Hoskuld is within."

The hamlet commander, Bors, held the door open. Gathelaus passed through with nary a look at the man and addressed Hoskuld who lay stewing in his misery at the dinner table. "Lord Hoskuld."

Hoskuld blinked and wiped his bloodshot eyes. "Gathelaus?"

"It's me."

Hoskuld remained seated, though it was plain to Gathelaus that he considered standing for his former king then thought better of it. He was lord here, and Gathelaus was no longer king. "I haven't seen you since your coronation in Hellainik. What brings you to my unhappy door?"

Gathelaus grinned at him like the devil. "You know why." He bowed slightly to a handful of women who eavesdropped from the far edge of the hall.

"You come to bring more misery to my hall?" accused Hoskuld, his shouts echoing in the near empty room. "We sent you our sons and they died defending you from a wizard, that I was later told you slew single handedly. Is that true? Makes the deaths of our sons seem pointless, doesn't it?" Before Gathelaus could answer, Hoskuld continued bitterly, "Regardless, the usurper was usurped and the new king, Vikarskeid, considers me and my folk little better than your other back woods lackeys. We are taxed beyond our means, and then on top of that, the dragon which has slept since the time of my grandfather's father, wakes and does evil on our land, so that we might all die of starvation and never see the halls of the slain."

Gathelaus stood silent and listened. Niels watched the hall warily, wondering if the few men Hoskuld had left might suddenly rush them for revenge, but none moved.

Hoskuld wept, saying, "Why are you here? Will you deny these things? Will you try and trade apologies for blood? Scorn for tears?"

Gathelaus proclaimed, "I will not. Your sons died defending me against a wizard that I avenged them for. Vikarskeid I will see dead one day soon, and for now, I am here to slay the dragon that curses your lands."

Hoskuld buried his head in his hands, saying sarcastically, "I'm thankful, I really am, but there isn't a thing any man can do. So you may as well see yourself out. Fall on your sword for all the good it will do. That might bring a smile to my face one last time."

"I've met some of your folk, I have seen the dragon. I will find a way."

Hoskuld shook his head. "You are deluded Gathelaus, old Usurper King, I had the last company of warriors I could command try and stand against Fiendal." He stood from his table and emphasized, swinging his fists. "Not a sword edge or spear point could penetrate his skin. Not an arrow, nor a burning torch did slow his terrible step. You'd get farther with your teeth against an oak than with an axe against his scales. You cannot slay that which cannot die." He paused amidst tears, muttering, "He took away my wife and my sons. He even took my leg." He peeled back a bit of his robe revealing a wooden leg. "All I have left is a daughter."

"Everything dies, even gods and monsters," answered Gathelaus.

"Perhaps, but for today we have almost no sheep left. We'll have no wool, no mutton, no clothes, and the deaths of gods will pale before frozen children," said Hoskuld bitterly.

"I am here to do what I can."

Hoskuld pointed at the door. "I'm ruined, and you had best leave this cursed valley before you join all my people that are dead. This Fiendal, a true demon beast of hell ... he took four men in the bunkhouse night before last. Good warriors, loyal thanes all. Please, just leave my hall. I care not anymore for hope or promises. The world I know has gone to hell."

Gathelaus answered him, "The world may go to hell, but that is no excuse for good men."

Hoskuld harrumphed at that and said, "I cannot ask anymore of anyone."

"You are not asking, I'm offering. You say that Fiendal cannot be pierced, poisoned, or cut." Gathelaus sat down across from Hoskuld and scratched his stubbled chin. "But there is always a way. And I will find it."

Bors proclaimed, "You heard right. Nothing more can be done. You best head on out. I know you've been considered an invincible hero to a whole lot of men, but that's only men who are fools. Besides, Vikarskeid got rid of you and Fiendal is far worse than any man."

Gathelaus looked at him coolly. "I'll deal with Vikarskeid as I already told your lord, *after* I slay your dragon."

FURY \ \ \ JAMES ALDERDICE

Bors persisted, "This is different. This thing is a wicked curse from the gods. There isn't anyone alive who knows how to kill such a thing as this."

Gathelaus took hold of a wine bottle from before Hoskuld and downed a great draught before answering, "Killing's an instinct for good or bad. One of the only talents I've got. I'll find a way."

"Can't be done," Bors taunted as he strode around the gloomy hall. "Gathelaus, you may have quite a reputation as a blood thirsty killer, but I have no doubt most of those slain were met with a knife in the back. I heard about you in Tolburn with your company of Sellsword's. You and a man named Gunnar ran that company of cut throats, and what happened to Gunnar?"

Hoskuld grumbled, "Enough Bors."

"No, it's all right," said Gathelaus. "Go on and tell it since you know the tale so well, friend."

Bors wiped his thin beard, answering, "I will. You served in the Kathulian wars under Gunnar, some minor prince paid you to usurp the throne for him. Funny how that is always your way. So you and Gunnar's men went to Kathul to arrange this informal coronation of the lost prince."

Gathelaus nodded. "True enough."

"Then one night Gunnar was horribly murdered. Seems just a day or so later, you up and fled from the palace in Kathul and you also inherited his command of the mercenaries. Pretty suspicious. You think any of that was bad, let me tell you something … this here

… is gonna be a whole lot worse." He gestured all around to drive home the point.

"You talk a lot of rot for a drunk. I took bloody handed vengeance on those that murdered Gunnar. They're dead and buried like anyone else that ever crossed me, and all of them had sword cuts in the front. Everyone knows my record as a mercenary captain, as well as that I took care of those wizards in Aldreth and their giant basilisk. I've already wrought vengeance on the wizard that stole the sons of this land. And there's still plenty of tales I have never told anyone from far across the sea. But in all my years of travel, I don't recall ever hearing any such tales of courage about you around the campfire, except maybe the one about why you're still alive but none of your lord's sons are, friend."

Bors frowned and slunk away amidst the giggling of the women folk.

"You might've been too hard on him," said Hoskuld, limping forward. "He's a good captain of the guard."

"Sometimes barking dogs need a kick."

Hoskuld nodded but said nothing as he lit his long pipe. Outside, the rain pelted the windows with an incessant rapping and the trees swayed against the wind. Gathelaus sensed a dark aura hanging over Finnsburg that had leeched the will power from its inhabitants.

Hoskuld said at last, "My sons were brave men, fighting to the last against an unstoppable killing machine. Would that I had been taken instead of them."

"I grieve with you Lord, but for now our responsibility is to the living. Tell me more about this Fiendal."

Hoskuld puffed on his pipe, sending smoke rings over his head like dirty halos. "It's big. Big as an elephant. Pear shaped body. Walks on two legs, large as great tree trunks, has a mighty tail that swings around like a thunderbolt, used that to knock my palace walls down. The arms are tiny, have claws but they are not to be feared. It's the mouth. A massive snake-like head with a maw full of bristling teeth, big as buffalo horns. Could swallow a man whole if it wanted, but usually it tears them apart first. It's gruesome I tell you. It does most of its killing with its mouth, some with the feet, but it's usually that awful fang sprouted mouth."

"Wings or fire-breathing?" asked Gathelaus, glancing a look at Niels, who stood by attentive and quiet.

"No, no wings nor fire breathing either, not that it matters in the path of such destruction. I suppose if it breathed fire all would have burnt to the ground by now, anything that has burned down was because it knocked our homes down on top of our cookfires," answered Hoskuld. "It is a demon."

Gathelaus listened and took another swallow from the wine bottle. "Sounds like a dragon to me. I have heard of wyrms that lived in the cold just like here."

Hoskuld agreed. "Legends have spoken of winged dragons and I've heard tales of fire breathers in the south lands, but I know only what I have experienced here. That is bad enough. We are cursed now."

"With every blessing comes a curse," said Gathelaus solemnly.

"I suppose it does. But while those other dragons in the south are considered reptiles and have scaly skin like Fiendal does, they're reptiles. Reptiles are dumb, but this monster is too smart for traps or poison. Fiendal isn't just any overgrown reptile. It looks reptilian for sure, but it's warm blooded."

Gathelaus cocked an eyebrow. "I thought you said no spear point or blade could pierce it."

"None ever have that I have seen. But I felt the thing once. That first night while it ate thirty of my men and a couple of the women from Hellainik, it pinned me against a dead horse and the barn. It was gulping down on some poor bastard and I felt its huge leg and it was warm. That tough scaly leg was warm! So, it's no dragon. It's a warm-blooded demon."

Gathelaus sketched a charcoal picture on a sheepskin and showed it to Hoskuld who had him shrink the arms even more.

"No, smaller. The arms are even smaller. No bigger than a big man's."

"How fast is it?"

"I think part of what makes it so dangerous is that it's warm blooded. I've been in the southlands in my youth and saw alligators moving slow when it was cold in the morning. Fiendal is never slow, he's been seen in the snow. No reptile could do that. So he's fast, can run faster than any horse. Votan's beard! If he is chasing a horse, he gets them, they're dead." He slammed his hands together to emphasize the point.

"How about this?" Gathelaus adjusted his drawing and Hoskuld nodded.

"You got it about right now."

"How about its senses? Eyes and ears, nose?" asked Gathelaus.

"Big eyes and nostrils, can't say I ever saw its ears but it sure isn't deaf. It doesn't like the sound of drums even if they can't hurt it. They angered him that first night. I swear before all the gods it was angry at our music, our singing, the drums and horns especially."

"Anything else you can tell me about it?"

Hoskuld went to cup his ears but stopped himself. "It roars, makes the most hideous sound you ever heard, like a hundred bears coming out of one cavernous mouth. It is the devil's mouthpiece."

Gathelaus pondered a moment longer and looked out the window toward the misty wilderness. "Every creature beds down sometime. Any ideas where Fiendal's lair might be?"

"Martin the priest, and a man-at-arms named Sturlang tracked it to the marshes against the north face. They said they guessed it went through the marsh to the caves on the other side. But ..."

"But what?" asked Gathelaus.

"They spoke about revenge, and the next morning they headed out after it with a pig stuffed with poison and powder kegs—the items I heard tell you used so admirably in Aldreth."

"What happened?"

Hoskuld continued, "We found what was left of them the next day. Hardly a grease spot, but Bors recognized Sturlang's hand and Martin's mangled lower legs near the marsh's edge. The poisoned pig was left behind, untouched. Fiendal could smell the poison."

"And the charges?"

"We heard them detonate just after dark, but whatever Martin and Sturlang tried, it did not wound or harm Fiendal and we had only those two charges. We have no more charges, and I have no more men. Despite our best efforts, men and livestock have been stripped away by Fiendal. More than half of the folk in my lands are dead or have fled. Of livestock left to us is less than half, perhaps not even one quarter."

"Can anything be done to trap the beast where it exits its home?"

"No, the marsh is too large. It is useless. We never went out that way again. We buried the hand and torso right there because of the worms."

Gathelaus sighed, "You are not giving me much to go on."

Hoskuld guffawed bitterly, "You know why? There isn't anything to give you. This demon spawn defies the gods with its very existence. This thing should not be. It's an abomination. I even spoke with the Pictish forest shaman, Curu-Calacht, and he said

Fiendal and his kin have been here since men came into the world. He said the demon owned this valley and that we were trespassing. He said we should just quit, leave. He said it would take a greater killer than the demon itself to win back this valley."

Gathelaus put his feet up on the table.

Hoskuld got up and looked out the window at his broken creation. "What can be done? We have sent more steel at that thing than we did at the Horde when they came over the mountains when I was young. The heavens no longer love us."

Gathelaus grinned. "You say blades don't work? Maybe I'll have to meet this monster head on without any swords or knives. Just so the gods pay attention again."

Hoskuld spun on Gathelaus, glaring. "The forest shaman said we should walk away. I cursed him for his advice. Walk away from all I and my forefathers have built up? I thought he was insane, and I pressed for us to hang on, thinking that someday we would slay the demon. But no one will come work for me anymore; the odds aren't in their favor of surviving. Over a hundred men have been slain these last twelve weeks. Bounties only brought death to more would-be heroes, and here you are proclaiming a weaponless plan?"

"I am the weapon."

"You're as insane as the monster. But maybe it takes a monster to kill a monster."

Gathelaus raised his wine bottle and took another swallow. "Maybe it does."

8. LAY OF THE LAND

The rain stopped, but a curling fog clung to the landscape like a death shroud. Somewhere in the distance an owl hooted, and the wind whipped off the pines sending needles spiraling. Up on the mountain peaks, the gusts pushed snow off the frozen stone like a comet's tail.

Gathelaus took Niels aside and asked, "Can you ride to wherever you think YonGee and other allies are?"

"Of course, but why not go together?"

"I must solve this puzzle and slay the monster," Gathelaus answered.

"You'll need all the help you can get," said Niels.

"Then hurry back with whoever you can muster," answered Gathelaus with a lop-sided grin.

"You want me to walk?"

Gathelaus withheld a chuckle. "They have horses in a stable set near a root cellar, I have already selected the swiftest one for you."

Niels shook his head with a laugh. "You want me to flee and leave you here?"

"You're coming back with all the loyal men you can muster."

"I don't know if it's enough for a dragon, judging by what Hoskuld has said."

"Come back anyway," said Gathelaus, clasping his friend's hand.

"I will as swiftly as I can," said Niels giving his exiled king a salute.

Gathelaus saw Niels off much to Bors consternation. If the grim aura didn't drape itself over the place, Gathelaus would have thought the land here beautiful. But before the sunset he wanted to have a personal understanding of the lay of the land. He asked the dozen men crowding around the false comfort of the fire ring, "Anyone willing to show me the way to the marsh?"

The men looked at him with barely concealed disgust.

"That's where the demon lives," said one, spitting a wad of tobacco.

"Fiendal is on the other side o' the swamp. You ought to go back where you came from, if you know what's good for you, usurper," said another, chortling.

Gathelaus exhaled loudly. "I want to see it. Someone just tell me the way."

A fat man with red sideburns rumbled, "You damned fool, we just told ya. You're asking for a pine box."

"No, he's asking to be dinner," another cackled.

Gathelaus wiped at his chin. "Just point me in the right direction. I don't need your concern."

"No!" shouted the first, spitting again. "You can't come here acting the hero. We all done our best and there ain't no such thing as heroes anymore. No one faces that rending demon and lives. You get on whatever sorry horse brought you here and go! We don't need you."

Gathelaus cocked his head at the man. "Now, that's just unfriendly."

The man spit his mouthful of black juice at Gathelaus's boots and grinned.

The hammer-like fist of Gathelaus hit the man square in the jaw, unhinging it. "Chew with your mouth closed."

The men gave a wide berth to Gathelaus as he stepped over the unconscious tobacco chewer on his way back to the stables. A boy feeding the horses said, "I can show you the way."

Gathelaus looked back at the men who would no longer meet his gaze. The chewer struggled to get off the ground. "That alright with your pa?"

The boy steeled himself before answering, "Fiendal ate my pa a fortnight ago." He then turned his face to brush away a tear.

"Sorry boy. You sure you wanna do this?"

Eyes blazing like dark burning embers, the boy answered, "Yes sir. I wanna see that monster fry in hell."

"Well, saddle up and I'll see what I can do."

† † †

"We only have a couple hours of daylight left boy. This isn't gonna be too far is it?"

The boy trotted his horse closer to Gathelaus. "No sir, it will not. I've only been to the marsh one time, but it wasn't far. Just over these hills and past those trees."

"Tell me boy, can you hear this Fiendal coming?"

"Sometimes yes, sometimes no. It can be sneaky. But it will growl and roar most of the time, so you usually have fair warning when he is a long way off. But some of the men must have been surprised because they never came back."

Gathelaus looked at him, nodding. "You're a brave boy."

They passed through a stand of aspens that grew close enough together they had to ride single file. The horses snorted and Gathelaus kept a vigilant eye out on either side of the trees, though it was difficult to see more than fifty feet.

"They smell something," said the boy.

"I do too," grunted Gathelaus. "The rot of the swamp and peat bog." Gathelaus dismounted and led his horse through the last of the trees to the grassy meadow that extended a hundred feet before hitting the swaying cattails.

There was a strange popping sound as if someone were cooking and there was a boil in a pot. Following the path of the stench, Gathelaus found a bubbling hot pot of tar or oil.

"Did you know about these?" he asked the boy.

"There are a few around the marsh and along this side of the mountains. I have heard the men say the oil pots are only on this side of the valley."

Gathelaus took a stick and jabbed at the black sticky substance. It was runnier than tar but very thick compared to an oil lamp. "Does anyone in Finnsburg burn this?"

"For outside lanterns, but it stinks, so no one uses it indoors."

Gathelaus nodded. "I may have you fetch a bucket or two full for me on the morrow."

"Yes, sir."

Fog wafted over the clearing and murky waters beyond. Behind the swamp loomed the titanic granite mountains. A cleft in the rock disappeared like a passageway into a mountainous tomb.

The boy shivered upon the back of his horse and pointed. "That is where the Fiendal lives."

Gathelaus handed the boy his reins and walked closer to the marsh. His boots sunk into the mud somewhat as he neared the staggered shoreline, and he knew the horses would sink worse than himself. But what about a creature the size of what he had been told? Sure enough a dozen paces to the south there was a cow path of sorts leading to a break in the reeds.

Except it wasn't a cow path.

Alternating each direction were tracks. There was no getting over the size of them. Massive three toed prints with a stride the length of a horse between them. They embedded several inches into the soft earth and were full of marsh water. Gathelaus looked closely and saw that the water was clean and still. These had to be at least a day old by his calculations. Each toe ended in a point, claws as big as his hand. Gathelaus looked toward the slot canyon in the mountain. He didn't hear anything but couldn't get over the feeling of being watched.

The mist had closed in some and the red glow of dusk stole over the mountains to the west, turning them black against the horizon.

"Maybe we ought to get back. We don't want to be caught out here after dark," said the boy softly.

Gathelaus nodded, watching the deep canyon across the marsh. "You're right, nothing more to learn here on our own."

The crack of lightning and subsequent thunder spooked the horses. The boy startled too and almost lost his grip on Gathelaus's reins.

"Easy, we're leaving. That was close."

But the boy's eyes were frozen, staring at the crest of the meadow to the south. He pointed, but while his mouth opened, nothing came out. Something moved through the fog. Shadowy and vague, it slipped between cascading banks of grey. A phantom just beyond recognition.

The hairs prickled and stood up on Gathelaus's forearms as he caressed the sword hilt at his side.

A tall grey figure moved beyond the edge of the hill, shrouded in fog. It came closer, slow and steady.

Gathelaus narrowed his gaze. The shape wasn't right. It was too short, too chaotic.

Parting through the mists revealed a red-skinned man. He was long past middling years. Gathelaus guessed he was the Pictish forest shaman, Curu-Calacht. His grey hair was fashioned in a braid and a few feathers clung, splayed down. He held a crutch like staff and silently lifted it toward Gathelaus.

"Curu-Calacht?"

The forest shaman gave what might either be a grimace or a smile. It was hard to tell because of his many wrinkles and lines. Curu-Calacht looked old as anyone living, his deep mahogany skin almost matched his buckskins. He also looked to the cleft and then ambled toward Gathelaus and the boy. "Not wise to be here now," he said slowly.

"You're here."

Curu-Calacht grunted. "I came to warn you. Let us get back to the hall." He tugged on Gathelaus's reins and swung his head in a demanding fashion.

"Take it easy old man. We were about to head back anyhow."

The old man grunted again.

"Boy, let him get on with you."

The boy fidgeted in his saddle and slid back a hand's breadth.

Curu-Calacht shrugged. "I can walk as fast as you can trot."

"Suit yourself. Let's get back into the trees and be on our way."

They slipped through the aspens but not before all of them stole another look back to the jagged cleft one last time. The stillness seemed to echo, and the foreboding was palpable.

"It is not safe to be near Fiendal's lair," repeated Curu-Calacht after they were beyond the aspens.

"Didn't think it was, but I wanted to learn all I could for myself. I saw his tracks, he's a big one," said Gathelaus, as he bit the end of a hunk of jerky.

Curu-Calacht grunted in agreement, then said, "He is very large, true, but he is not yet full grown. He is famished with growth now, that is why he has awoken and is eating so much. He feels the need in his bones. He must feed." The old forest shaman slapped himself in the chest as he himself felt the primal hunger he spoke of.

Gathelaus's eyebrows raised and he neglected to swallow. "Not full grown?" he muttered through his teeth clenching the strip of meat. "What do you mean? How do you know that?"

"It is the way of things, everything young grows larger," said the shaman matter-of-factly.

"No, how do you know he isn't full grown and just a ravenous monster?"

Curu-Calacht rubbed at his bare chin and pondered what to say a long moment. "Fiendal dwells with his mother and she was greater in size than he still. So, I am sure that he has the potential to be maybe," he paused and held his arms out wide at his sides as if guessing both length and what to say next. "I'd say twice as big as he is now." He nodded amiably.

Gathelaus tore the jerky from his own mouth. "You mean there are two of them? Hoskuld has only mentioned the one, nobody has said anything about a second."

The old shaman nodded. "I saw them hunting together many moons ago when I was a boy, this was long before your people settled here. They and the great thunderbirds dwelt here, but like all things, they change, die, and return to the earth. The age of heroes before the cataclysm destroyed most monsters that covered the earth, otherwise man could not be."

"But those two are still here?"

"Perhaps, but perhaps the mother has gone the way of all things and sleeps forever in the earth too. I do not know for certain."

"You almost sound disappointed."

Curu-Calacht moved his hand across the horizon and down. "I am sorry to see any creature's time pass. My time comes soon as well. I have lived much longer than most men. All is held in thrall by the hidden God that moves in all things. There is a season for all and for all, a passing."

"Even these monsters?" asked Gathelaus, indignant as he reached for another piece of jerky. Seeing the boy salivating, he tossed him one as well. The boy snatched at the meat and tore into it like a starving man.

Curu-Calacht said, "They had their place. But as man's civilization encroaches a deadly struggle comes. Old times clash with the new."

Gathelaus said, "Hoskuld told me you said this is Fiendal's valley."

"He was here first," said the old Pict with a shrug.

"He is a monster; he kills men and beasts."

Curu-Calacht raised a finger in the air. "Is he the monster, though? Or are—"

"Shut up! He is a dragon, he kills. I'll put him down the same as I would any pest that threatens innocent men," said Gathelaus.

Curu-Calacht shrugged.

Gathelaus sat on his horse and pondered the fissure in the mountain across the marsh from himself. "He is just better at it than most."

Curu-Calacht nodded sage. "The other men do not know how to kill Fiendal, but your aura, I can see you are blessed by the great invisible Spirit. You have the blessing way of doom, the instinct of killing and will surely find a way. I am sure."

"Thanks, I suppose. You don't have any more direct pointers, though do you?" He held out a piece of jerky to the old man who looked as hungry as did the boy.

The old man took Gathelaus's jerky and tore at it a moment before answering, "Look for death and you will find. Your old ways of the sword is not the way to succeed against such ancient enemies. As you made a boast of yourself, you shall be tested. Trust not in the arm of flesh but have faith in yourself and the great invisible Spirit's guidance." He then tried to hand back half of the strip of jerky.

Frowning, Gathelaus mumbled, "You can keep that."

Curu-Calacht nodded and finished devouring the strip of dried meat. "He will come hunting for you soon. Perhaps not tonight, though." He chewed thoughtfully. "He may go up valley after a swift horse, I heard one running earlier. Fiendal likes to chase horses. I think he likes the sport of the chase."

"Something tells me I ain't gonna be able to relax yet."

"No, you won't," agreed Curu-Calacht with a wry grin.

"With all you just told me, did you really come all the way out here just to warn me off?"

Curu-Calacht shrugged, grinning. "No, I also wanted some jerky."

9. DEMANDS AND THREATS

Back within Finnsburg's walls, they heard Fiendal roaring in the night, but he did not approach the Hall, though Gathelaus stayed awake almost all night waiting for him. All night long the tramp of doom sounded into the north end of the valley. Gathelaus guessed that Niels had to be long gone, but the concern for his friend still bore fruit that made for a restless night.

He slept late into the morning and finally awoke with a bright sun cascading through the torn curtains.

There was a clamor out front, so he got up to see what the matter was.

A wagon that had been pushed into place held the broken gates shut. The women rushed to help bar the way, their arms full of wreckage from Fiendal's destruction. The men were mounted above the gate with spears and bows in hand.

The boy raced up. "I was coming to wake you. Lord Hoskuld said you should see this."

"I'm coming," answered Gathelaus as he tightened his sword belt. He splashed water in his face from a rain barrel that had been overflowing until this morning, now that the showers had finally given them a break.

Hoskuld shouted, "I cannot answer your demands."

FURY \ \ \ JAMES ALDERDICE

Gathelaus heard another man shouting, this one sounded like he was outside the walls. "I know he is here. Dagoo, my Pictish tribesman speaks with the spirits and the spirits do not lie. They tell us Gathelaus is here."

Hoskuld stood upon the gate parapet and turning, saw Gathelaus's approach and called out, "Well, then, here he is now. Perhaps he will heed your call." He was speaking to someone on the other side of the wall. Likely as not the huntsmen had caught up to him.

Gathelaus made his way to the steps that would bring him up to the parapet.

Hoskuld took a step toward him and growled quietly, "I'm angry with you, but I'm not about to turn a former king out to these dogs."

Gathelaus wondered at that, but as he made his way up to see over the parapet, he was not terribly surprised. A dozen horsemen were arrayed there. All looked to be wild and vicious men. Their leader stood out as he still wore a hood and you could hardly see any of his face, just a clean-shaven chin. Beside him was a cruel looking little man with reddish skin, a Pict, likely kin to old Curu-Calacht. The rest of the riders looked as to be expected, a motley crew of warriors hungry for blood and gold.

"You must be Tarbona," said Gathelaus.

"That I am. And we all know your name, Usurper," answered Tarbona. "Will you spare these people you are hiding with bloodshed and come out? Surrender yourself to me and I'll treat you well all the way to Vikarskeid's palace. I swear it." He placed his hand over his heart but had a cruel smile upon his face.

"Afraid not. I don't see a horse meant for me to ride and I'll not be dragged all the way to Hellainik.

Tarbona glanced about as some of his men snickered. "You always were a bloody man, Gathelaus, letting others die for your sins," challenged Tarbona. "Hoskuld!" he cried.

"Within my own hall, I am Lord Hoskuld to you dog!" shouted Hoskuld.

"Seems a poor kingdom you have for yourself then," rebuked Tarbona. "Do you know how much gold King Vikarskeid is offering for the usurper's head? I dare say enough to turn your sorry life around. Tell you what. Send him out to us and I'll give you all the gold I have in my satchel. More than a hundred crowns.

"All you have to do is open your gate and let us take him. I know he is surly. Slew almost a dozen of my men back in the fishing village of Bjornsburg."

So that was the name of that fishing village, Gathelaus realized. He would have to tell Niels.

Gathelaus said, "Credit where credit is due, Tarbona. I slew four outside the tavern and then two more inside, Niels inside slew the other four or five."

"You both crippled three, but together slew ten," answered Tarbona. "I know how to count my men."

"I do not take demands from bandits at my wall, Tarbona!" shouted Hoskuld, "No matter how many false promises they give."

Tarbona laughed and reached into his saddlebags. He produced a stout leather sack and withdrew from it a handful of gold coins that gleamed in the morning sunlight. "I keep my word Lord Hoskuld. Give me Gathelaus and I'll give you these and more. If you're frightened of his famed ferocity, simply just open your gates and stay out of our way. We'll bring him to heel one way or another."

Some of Hoskuld's men murmured their agreement at the proposed bargain, but Hoskuld answered him. "I fear I cannot accept your terms, bandit chief. I think if I opened my gates to you; that you would take the man and give me a knife in the back for my troubles. There is precious little justice in the world, but I have opened my doors to the former king Gathelaus, and he shall remain safe here so long as I am lord of Finnsburg."

"Then it seems I have another goal and that one I shall do for free," threatened Tarbona.

"Back you dogs!" shouted Bors, as he drew back on his bow. "Leave off or I swear I shall strike you down first!"

Tarbona laughed. "We shall leave, but this isn't over." He signaled his men and they rode back down the way they had come. Last of all was the little red man who squinted at Gathelaus and gave him a curious salute of respect.

FURY ✝ ✝ ✝ JAMES ALDERDICE

The men of Finnsburg grumbled on the wall but Hoskuld said, "I have taken you in and I will not turn you out, but for my peace and that of my remaining folk, perhaps you should leave soon. Go meet up with your kinsman that left yesterday, and I will say no more in angry words to you. The words you said yesterday will be forgotten and I forgive your failings as no man can rid me of the dragon and the doom that has come upon my house."

Gathelaus looked the lord of Finnsburg in the eye saying, "I'm not going anywhere, Hoskuld, until I have slain that dragon, then I will ride on and slay Vikarskeid and I will be king of this land again."

Hoskuld shook his head. "Men hunger for your blood. I can't hold those huntsmen from my hall, damnit I can't even hold a dragon from my hall. They will come and claim you in the night if the dragon doesn't first."

"I'll kill them all if I have to."

"Bold words, boldly spoken, but you're not a usurper king commanding armies anymore," chided Hoskuld with a sniff as he pulled at his beard. "I have more men than you and I cannot hold back the wolves from door come nightfall, let alone a dragon."

Gathelaus said, "I told you what I would do, and I will do it. Just keep your folk safe in the meantime. I will deal with these wolves soon enough."

"Bors and the others can be counted on to keep watch along the wall for Tarbona, but if they hear the dragon coming, they will flee to their holes and I do not fault them. Nothing can slay that monster."

"My thanks, but I will deal with Tarbona and his huntsmen as well."

Hoskuld clapped Gathelaus on the shoulder, saying, "I will defend you, but I don't want any more harm coming to my folk."

Gathelaus said, "Tarbona's men are not expecting a dragon. They won't attack in broad daylight and come nightfall the dragon may as likely come after them outside the walls before coming here again. Don't you think?"

Hoskuld grinned. "That would be a poetic fix for him and his dreaded huntsmen to find themselves in, but I worry it may not come as soon as I would like."

"Is that a worry or do you have some knowledge?"

Hoskuld said, "Fiendal seems to range sections of the valley. It is not always so, but we have noticed a pattern that he usually follows. He did the south two nights ago, the north yesterday and tonight he will do the east. Tarbona's men camp in the south and will not likely be molested by the dragon. Instead they will raid us, likely firing the hall and the rest of our homes that the dragon has left standing."

Gathelaus wondered at that. "Unless I can bring the dragon to them."

Hoskuld shook his hoary head. "The saying is right, only a madman would seek to be a king."

10. THE DOOM LADEN TRAIL

Gathelaus offered to pay the boy a silver coin to sneak off into the trees, covering himself in mud and vines, that he might be able to spy a little closer to where Tarbona and his huntsmen encamped. The hesitation of the boy wasn't fear but in the payment.

With a grin, Gathelaus fished some more jerky out of his saddlebags for the boy, who was more interested in food than coin.

"Be cautious, don't let them see or hear you and don't get closer than a bowshot away. Understand?"

The boy nodded and hurried away, clutching the jerky like a rare prize.

He would not have bid the boy do such a thing if he believed any real danger would befall him but told him to stay far from their sight and only to report their possible comings and goings before nightfall.

The boy wanted to help but was nervous, and Gathelaus assured him that he should not stay out spying beyond twilight. The boy agreed and stalked off into the thick grass and then the trees separating the hamlet's wall from where Tarbona was.

The bounty hunter captain had chosen a spot not far away from the walls of Finnsburg. It was secluded in thick trees but had a good view of the road which led to Finnsburg and beyond. Any rider would be seen as well as heard, even in the night, unless he should cover his horse's hooves with rags.

Tarbona took no chances, sending a pair of men farther up the road to wait and watch. Two men would not be a challenge for a swordsman so renowned as Gathelaus, but these men also ran a cold camp with no fire and had horns to blast warning for the others in case of alarm.

Gathelaus guessed that Tarbona would move his camp in the night if not do a full-blown assault on Finnsburg. It was very possible he had kept some of his men back and only revealed a dozen to test Hoskuld's resolve. It's what he would have done. Never let the enemy know your true strength and numbers.

At dusk, the boy returned saying that two men were waiting beside the road under a thicket of trees in a sheltered glade, but just as the sun dipped below the mountains, another two came up from behind them, doubling their number on the watch. He said they spoke softly, so he didn't know what was said, but that they seemed anxious.

Gathelaus wondered if Tarbona would do a frontal assault after dark or wait until nearly morning when the folk would be unable to see an attacker on the dark ground contrasted with the lightening sky of dawn. According to the boy, the huntsmen he had seen had spent the day napping as if to be well rested come nightfall.

Guessing that would be their plan, Gathelaus decided he would take the fight to them before they could attack him as well as Hoskuld's folk.

So, he armed himself with a bow, a dozen shafts, and his sword and axe. He was readying himself to slip out through a broken chink in the wall, when Curu-Calacht stopped him.

"You are here to fight the dragon for these people. Yet these men come saying you are the evil one with a price on your head."

"You heard that, huh?" Momentarily, Gathelaus wondered if the old Pict was hoping to collect that reward himself, he fingered his knife hilt, ready to thrust forward if necessary.

"But I say, you do the right thing. Let me go take care of these men and send them far from here. Their greed can be sated with blood if they will not go."

"I can fight my own battles," argued Gathelaus.

Curu-Calacht pressed a firm hand against Gathelaus's chest and he was surprised at the sheer power the old man possessed. "This dragon is not your battle and yet here you are to try and safeguard these peoples."

"Got to do what I can."

Curu-Calacht nodded and said, "A proud man can give but he will not ask. Let me help you."

"All right. You done this before, chief?" asked Gathelaus.

Curu-Calacht simply turned and gave Gathelaus the coldest look he had ever seen, something about those eyes was almost repellant.

Gathelaus watched the old man stride soft as a shadow into the tall grass, silent as a ghost. In no time he could no longer see nor hear the old man. Even the grass where he guessed the old man must be moving appeared no more disturbed than if a light breeze was blowing across the tall yellow stalks.

Gathelaus then worried—what if the old man was only remembering his glory days of youth? Perhaps he had been a great warrior decades ago and was now just trying to go out with a glorious last battle. He rushed through the grass after the old man. He remained as stealthy as he could but supposed that soon he would hear a struggle and the old man would be captured and tortured by the huntsmen. He hurried along the path, with his knife out ready to slam it into the foe.

But as he cleared the roadway and the moon danced out from behind the clouds, he heard a terrible sound.

A deep guttural wolf's howl split the sky followed by the sudden fearful cry of men about to die. Their horses, which had been picketed only softly in the wet turf, broke free and fled in a desperate panic.

Gathelaus recognized the sound of a blade being drawn and slamming into a tree as it missed its intended target. The fresh gurgle of blood as a throat was torn out.

"Please, no," whimpered a man, but it was answered with only bestial snapping.

FURY ≻ ≻ ≻ JAMES ALDERDICE

The awful sound of slashing claws and splashed blood filled the glade where the men had hidden. Bones crunched and Gathelaus heard a wicked slurping sound as if marrow were being drawn.

He worried if the wolfshead thing had come and while it had devoured his enemies the huntsmen, what about the old Pict? What about himself?

"Curu?" he whispered.

The sound of a loud sniff carried across the glade and Gathelaus heard bipedal paws loping away. Pressing forward with both his sword and dagger drawn, he glanced warily at the bloody ruin within the glade. Four men had been torn apart. It had happened so suddenly that he didn't think the sleeper had even awoken before death took him. Perhaps that was a better way to go than final seconds of horror.

"Curu-Calacht," he whispered urgently again. But there was no answer. He stole back to Finnsburg, guessing at the wolfish accessory.

On his way there he heard Fiendal off in the distance roaring his displeasure, perhaps he smelled the blood on the air and knew it was not his doing, but that there was another predator around.

Back at the walls he kept a sharp lookout for not only Tarbona, but Curu-Calacht and the wolfshead.

Soon he heard the disquiet from Tarbona's men as they moved through the darkness and discovered what had happened to their four outliers. They also heard the dragon and muttered among themselves that it was some kind of trick.

Tarbona gave a near silent order, commanding an attack. "Onward!"

If Gathelaus hadn't been in the right position on the parapet, so close to where the bloody glade was, he didn't think he would have heard the order. But he heard the quick thunder of hooves well enough.

Four men on horseback came charging toward the far left of the gatehouse, while the other four raced to the far right.

They shot fire arrows at the gate, which stuck fast in the wagon. But being soaked from the snow and rain, this amounted to nothing. A score of flaming arrows were loosed over the wall to try and burn whatever they might strike too. The huntsmen were unaware that almost everything that could burn had already done so, thanks to the dragon's previous destruction.

The handful of fire arrows they shot at the wagon of a gate, were easily extinguished by a pair of wall wardens.

The assault was one of the more pathetic displays Gathelaus had ever been a witness to.

One of the riders came too close to the gatehouse and was doused by one of the wall wardens with a privy bucket. The foul rider swore and rode away, puking and almost falling out of his own saddle. And just as soon as it had begun it was over, the eight riders retreated, without losing a man in the attempt, though one had lost all his dignity.

Hoskuld limped out to see what had happened.

"They came and staged a half-hearted assault on the walls and were easily repelled," said Gathelaus.

Hoskuld's men cheered, thinking they had beat back a great assault from a sieging force, but Gathelaus scolded them. "Don't celebrate too soon. That was all for show. They were probing to see what defenses we have."

Bors argued, "And if you weren't here there wouldn't be a need for any of this."

Hoskuld reprimanded him. "I gave the order. Gathelaus is my former lord and I will not turn him over to anyone on threat of my person or my people. I don't want to hear another word against him."

Gathelaus continued, "The real attack will come swift and savage nearer dawn I should think, once they think our guard is down."

"What about the dragon?" asked a wall warden.

Hoskuld said, "If the gods bless us with any luck, Fiendal would deal with the huntsmen."

They waited and the Tarbona's riders made another attempt to circumnavigate the walls and ride through the breach where Gathelaus had crept out to spy upon the dead men, but as soon as one of the men took an arrow to the throat, they abandoned this attempt too.

The dragon roared now, from somewhere north of the hall, and Gathelaus watched as the huntsmen panicked, wondering if it were all a trick of sorts. A sorcerous call meant to make them give up the attack.

Tarbona called it a trick and urged his men to regroup in the trees.

Soon thereafter, they all heard Fiendal come prowling through passes and the terror from Tarbona's men was no longer withheld.

Gathelaus heard the mighty tramp of doom as the dragon loped its way toward Finnsburg. The night was dark, and the clouds had rolled back over the moon. He heard the huntsmen cry out and the horses, too, screamed in terror as the monster ran down the slope at them.

Shapes were black and speeding in the dark but there was no doubt they were witness to terrible carnage outside the walls of Finnsburg. The wall wardens watched in abject fright, at once grateful that the monster was feeding upon their enemies and not themselves. But still they remained ready to run at the first sign that the dragon might turn its attention back toward the walled hamlet.

Fiendal ran down the men and horses in the gloom. The sound of rending flesh, snapping bones, and greedy gulping bites was a terrible thing to hear when you could not see.

Hoskuld said to the wall wardens, "It is an ill thing to see that doom come to your enemies, but I am glad that just this once, the dragon spared my own folk from bloodshed."

The men climbed down off the walls and hurried to their deep hiding places in case the dragon should approach the walls. None of them wished to be noticed by it.

Gathelaus and Hoskuld were the last, each scanning the dark, listening to the carnage.

"I don't think we will be worrying anymore about those huntsmen," said Hoskuld.

Gathelaus grunted his agreement. "Have you seen Curu-Calacht?"

"The Pict shaman? Not tonight, but he moves like a ghost. He is the swiftest old man I have ever seen."

"Anything else strange about him?"

Hoskuld shrugged his broad shoulders. "Besides that he is a Pict? And a hundred years old. No."

"Never any problems with him?" asked Gathelaus.

"With the Picts? Not since the days of my grandfathers when they drove his people out of the valley and into the mountains. I heard tales of bloody raids against the fort, but that was all over before I was born. Most of his kind died off or moved away. Like the dragon, he is the last of his kind here."

They listened once more as Fiendal tramped farther to the south and eventually they heard him no more.

False dawn teased at the horizon and Hoskuld said, "I will go offer libations to the gods for sparing my house but not my enemies this night."

"I didn't know you were a praying man."

"The dragon has made all men remember the gods," said Hoskuld. "But you're right, I wasn't always this way. My daughter reminded me that I could still do this when I can do nothing else."

"Your daughter? Is she?"

"She still lives. But I sent her away. She is the last of my line and I wanted to know she was safe. She is a hellcat, though, and fought me tooth and nail. Wanted to stay here. You know she prayed to the gods weeks ago, asking that a killer like you might arrive to slay the fiend. Maybe she was right," mused Hoskuld.

11. SONG OF TREACHERY

Come daybreak they saw the bare destruction of Tarbona's men. A horrific red smear on the ruin of tall grass not two hundred yards from the gatehouse was all that remained of Tarbona's huntsmen. It was difficult to tell what was man or beast, but it was clear there were several mangled carcasses among the gut piles. Even the men that had been slain by the wolfshead farther up the road had been partially devoured.

"I believe I heard several of the men racing away in the dark. I don't think Fiendal got them all, or if he did, it would have been miles from here," said one of the wall wardens.

"And if anything could run them down, it would be Fiendal, the bastard!" said Bors.

Gathelaus sensed Bors gazing at him. The captain of Hoskuld's men glared angrily over the top of his jack of ale.

Bors continued speaking low to his men, but not so quiet that Gathelaus could not hear him. "Then maybe soon, we can collect some reward ourselves to make up for our ill luck thus far, maybe then—"

Hoskuld slapped a hand down on Bors' shoulder and squeezed. He leaned in to whisper into his headman's ear menacingly. "Anymore such talk against my guest and you will be put out to pasture in a box. Am I understood?"

"Yes, my lord, I just wanted—"

"No more. It isn't wise to taunt a man that slays for a living," said Hoskuld as he limped away and joined Gathelaus at his solitary table.

Gathelaus raised his ale mug in silent greeting.

Hoskuld said, "Please do not hold my wayward servants accountable for their foolish words. I have few enough men as it is."

Gathelaus grunted, sipped his ale, then said, "I'll let any words go by, but if a blade is raised in my direction …"

Hoskuld gave a withering glare toward Bors. "You have my blessing if it comes to that."

"I hope for your folk's sake it doesn't. You have few enough men as it is."

Hoskuld smirked and grimly nodded. "True. He and Brotheus are my last most resolute men."

Gathelaus asked, "I prepare to face the dragon. Is there anything I can count on?"

"There is a pattern in all things the dragon does. He seems to wander differing parts of the valley every few days and so we know which nights he will come. Barring something unusual, he shouldn't come to Finnsburg tonight, but the next night."

"He is that predictable?"

Hoskuld gave pained smile. "I wouldn't call it that, but it is a routine now. We know what nights will be the worst. We have learned it with blood these last few weeks."

"So, I have some time to prepare?"

Hoskuld stood from the table and spoke loudly enough for his men to hear. "Yes, anything at my disposal that you can utilize you have my blessing for acquisition."

"Thank you, Lord Hoskuld. I will begin my preparations in earnest."

"Anything," said Hoskuld with a wave of his hand. He glanced at Bors, saying curtly, "Anything."

Bors bowed his head to Hoskuld then approached Gathelaus asking, "How can I be of service to you?"

Gathelaus rubbed at his chin, asking, "Tell me where the blacksmith shop is and where I can get the longest rope possible."

Bors answered him, "I will fetch the ropes, but the blacksmith shop was destroyed the first night the dragon came. We still have most of the tools though. They were recovered and are now kept out of the rain among the stables. But we have no functioning bellows nor a working furnace for metal working."

"That's fine. I may only want to use a few of the tools."

Bors gave a half-hearted salute and walked away.

The rest of the morning, Gathelaus stalked over the courtyard of the hamlet, taking his own measurements and judging the strength and weight of various stones and blocks from the ruins of the palace. He sent the boy to fetch a few buckets of the tar-like oil and had these placed at strategic points around the courtyard.

Once Bors brought him the ropes, Gathelaus wound and connected several ropes together to make a long line that he hoped might be capable of tripping the dragon. He didn't think that any of the rope he had could hold it. He dug a shallow trench to cover where he would conceal it between two points. It was a gamble if it could be done, but tripping the monster up was only one of several plans he had going forth to level his chances against what everyone said was an invincible demon.

Curu-Calacht arrived sometime later after noon. He had several blood smears across his cheek, chest, and forehead, but Gathelaus could tell it was not his own blood.

Gathelaus greeted him, saying, "Seems you handled those huntsmen just fine."

"They were no trouble, but there was something else out there last night," said the old Pict.

"Did *it* cause you any trouble?"

The old Pict shook his head with a subtle grin. "No. When the time comes, I will stand with you."

"Thank you," said Gathelaus.

"But that won't be tonight" said Curu-Calacht. "Fiendal hunts the south-east of the valley tonight. But tomorrow, he comes here." He tapped a finger to his eyes and made as if he were surveying the whole of the inner hamlet.

"Thanks," said Gathelaus, skeptically.

The old Pict turned and walked away. That was apparently all he needed to say.

Gathelaus finished his preparations after a few hours and made ready for something to eat. As he sat outside on a stump, the wagon was rolled out from the gatehouse.

"Who is here?" he asked the boy.

The boy shrugged but ran to see who was coming, he reached the parapet, then came racing back. "People seeking refuge," he said.

Within a few moments several wagons and more people and animals than they could hold rolled into the courtyard. The wall wardens seemed familiar with a few of the men leading the wagons, so Gathelaus decided they wouldn't likely be any of the huntsmen of Tarbona, but still he asked the boy, "Do you know those people?"

The boy nodded. "That's Gil Hrut and his family, and the bearded man beside him is Rognar. I don't know those other two men though. They are strangers."

The boy pointed at a very tall mustachioed man in a black cloak with a brown tri-corner hat. He wore fancy boots, had a silver rapier at his side, and carried a lute across his back. It was the same lone bard he had seen at the crossroads.

The other man was even taller and looked travel worn wearing ill-fitting, ragged clothing and it was not immediately apparent who or what he was. He had a shock of blond hair and a reddish beard making him appear to be an Azschlander, but he did have a fine sword that Gathelaus's trained eye told him was well used, a true fighting man's blade.

One of the refugee farmers spoke aloud to Bors, "We have no more sulphur to ward off the dragon. We hoped we might come here for the sake of a safe place with you."

Bors replied, "We'll make room one way or the other, but we are nearly out ourselves. But then again," as he stole a glance toward Gathelaus, "we have a hero who thinks he can slay the dragon."

The farmer glanced at Gathelaus, though he didn't understand the sarcastic implication of Bors' words. "Who is that?"

Bors whispered, "The Usurper."

"The king!" spat the farmer. "Here?"

The tall man with the lute and the even taller yet ragged fighting man looked Gathelaus's way at the revelation. They then looked to one another and approached him. The ragged man with a noticeable limp.

Gathelaus stood, unsure of their intentions and wondering if they might be more hired men, looking to gain wealth at the expense of his name.

The bard and the ragged man noticed Gathelaus's wary stance and they held their arms apart from their weapons. The bard spoke first, "King Gathelaus, I am Brodir, a skald of some renown. Perhaps you have heard of me? As I know you are a lover of truth and freedom, let me say that I am your man." He then knelt on one knee before Gathelaus, awaiting his reaction.

"Rise Brodir, the world could always use another good skald. And you Azschlander?"

The ragged man did not kneel but lowered his head, saying, "Forgive me if I do not kneel, but I had a bad fall with a horse last night and my leg might not let me back up. I am Hunwulf. I have been many things in my time. But as you can see," as he patted the hilt of his sword, "I don't plant wheat."

Gathelaus asked, "And you'll not tell me that you are my man like the skald?"

Hunwulf chuckled. "Honestly, I thought you were dead until just recently. Besides, you're not king anymore, but we all have our ups and downs. I'd just as soon have a friend of you if you'll have me. I imagine your fortunes will rise again soon, eh?"

Gathelaus nodded. "I'm working on that."

"Any chance, you would like help with this dragon slaying business then?" asked Hunwulf. "I wouldn't mind making a name for myself in that effort."

"You've heard the odds?"

Hunwulf laughed. "If you're still standing here, I reckon you have a plan. Not many men would willingly face a dragon. I think I am with the skald and want to attach my sword to your train, if you'll have me."

"Well met," said Gathelaus, and they shook hands.

Brodir took hold of the lute and strummed, singing aloud,

"Well met warriors in Vjornishtown,

Plans to take the dragon down,

A skald, a fighter and a king,

All together what doom we'll bring.

Fangs of steel and breath of fire,

Hotter than a maiden's desire!"

The last line caused Gathelaus to become aware of a beautiful maiden who had just arrived on horseback behind the wagon train. She was shapely and pale with long black hair. He recognized her as the barmaid from Bjornsburg. The very same one that Niels had been speaking of. But what was she doing here?

Brodir saw that Gathelaus was no longer paying attention. "Well, I did just make it up on the spot, but I can improve the beginning."

"It's Finnsburg, not Vjornishtown," said Hunwulf.

"There aren't any good rhymes with Finnsburg!" protested Brodir.

"Bah!" growled Hunwulf.

Gathelaus stepped forward and watched the woman dismount. She seemed aware of the place and not surprised at the destruction of the palace or state of disrepair upon the rest of the hamlet. One of the wall wardens greeted her warmly and with noted subservience.

The sound of the lute hitting the ground gave Gathelaus pause.

Gathelaus was watching her when he caught her eye and she shouted, "Behind you! That's Tarbona's man!"

Gathelaus wheeled just as the point of the thrusting blade licked forth and skittered across his mail along the ribs. Had he not moved, the point would surely have had the sheer power to penetrate and perhaps touch his heart.

Hunwulf snarled in disappointment.

"You come for the king, you best not miss," challenged Gathelaus, as he drew his own blade.

Brodir was on the ground, a stab wound in his side gushing blood.

Bors and the woman as well as the other folk crowded closer, though not too close as Gathelaus and Hunwulf began their duel.

Their blades slammed together and apart in the delicate dance of death. It was clear that each man was a master of the sword. As they drew back and relaunched their attack, Gathelaus slashed through some of Hunwulf's ragged cloak, revealing fine black mail beneath.

Hunwulf in turn, kicked at Gathelaus as they broke apart. He taunted, "You're almost as good as my commander, Tarbona."

Gathelaus snorted. "Is he dead then?"

They crossed blades once again and the tip of Hunwulf's sword came perilously close to Gathelaus's eye. "No, but I wanted to try and claim your head myself. More reward that way."

"Hard to spend that pay in hell," growled Gathelaus as he pressed the foe back, his blade a slicing fury of steel.

Hunwulf groaned under the impact as he blocked. The blades rang together in discordant song. "I'll eat your heart!"

"You wouldn't be the first man to try."

Hunwulf snarled, "But I'll be the last!" He charged in swinging a terrible arc, but Gathelaus sidestepped and slashed a deep cut against Hunwulf's exposed left hand.

"No bad horse fall last night?" asked Gathelaus.

"Your taunts won't work, usurper," Hunwulf said with a sniff. "No, but I did lose almost all of my company thanks to you. I would never have thought you a sorcerer to conjure a werewolf and dragon as well."

"I'm no sorcerer," said Gathelaus, as their blades rang together. "But you don't know the dangers that stalk this land."

Blades sparked like flint against steel lighting a fire of hatred against one another, they stepped apart to temper the forging process.

"We tracked you this far. You won't get away," said Hunwulf.

"I hope the wolf got your Pictish tracker."

Hunwulf shook his head. "Dagoo? He's too wily for that."

A quick sweep and stroke forward brought both to a shuddering standstill. Deep notches in Hunwulf's blade betrayed who had the finer steel.

"But I was thrown by your look, I didn't recognize you from yesterday at the gates."

Hunwulf laughed mirthlessly. "A man in my line of work must have many tricks up his sleeve." He reached for a dagger at his belt.

"Your work ends here," growled Gathelaus as he pressed forward and slashed along Hunwulf's sword arm. Several of the links sheared and his mail was dyed red.

Switching his blade to his other already wounded hand, Hunwulf eyed any possible avenue of escape. Finding none, he cursed his fate, "Mahmackrah take your heart!" He charged forward, swinging like a man possessed.

Gathelaus cast aside the initial blow and swept his sword back across Hunwulf's neck cords, sundering his windpipe.

Hunwulf's eyes bulged in horror, the sword fell from his fist and his knees buckled. He could not speak, but his dying eyes cast terrible woe at Gathelaus. Then he fell back and was still.

"Thanks for that," said Brodir with a cough. "Now, can someone, please, staunch this flow?"

12. MORALS AND DOGMA

As both Curu-Calacht and Hoskuld had said, Fiendal made no appearance that night, though they did hear his roar far off to the east and south. Whenever he cried, any livestock including the dogs and cats about the hamlet would go silent. Everything knew what the true predator was, and none wanted its attention.

In the morning, Gathelaus checked his preparations again. All was as set as he could make it. He hoped Niels would be back soon, but it was a long way to Hellainik, and any number of troubles could befall his returning with more loyal men.

He went to check on the skald Brodir who had been moved into one of the root cellars as a precautionary measure against whenever the dragon would arrive. The stairwell door was open and a woman with long brunette hair left, carrying a basin filled with bloody bandages. She smiled at Gathelaus as she passed him on the steps. He heard Brodir inside calling out, "Where are you off to lass, have you not heard me sing The Lion of Misty Eurie?"

"I have twice now," she called back. She looked to Gathelaus and said, "He has been drinking more ale than he should for the pain."

"Brodir, will you survive?" Gathelaus asked, as he descended the stairs.

Hoskuld was there already. He greeted Gathelaus and said, "Brodir is not about to die but will be in no condition to stand beside you tonight. He can't even roll over."

"Is that what you called it?" teased Brodir.

"It looked like he had a good nurse," said Gathelaus.

Hoskuld said, "Aye, Sari knows a thing or two about wounds."

Brodir laughed as he also grimaced in pain. "I've had worse. Thank the gods, that bastard didn't cut my fingers though, at least I can still play so long as I don't bend too much."

"It's a miracle."

"It is," said Brodir as he flexed his fingers and lithely ran them up and down the frets of the lute. "And miracles offend unbelievers." He handed the lute to Hoskuld.

Hoskuld took it but rolled his eyes.

"About that bastard, where did you meet the man who called himself, Hunwulf?" Gathelaus asked.

"I was bound swiftly away from Danelaw, as a certain set of lawyers didn't take kindly to my mocking them in the town square."

"You've known him since?" asked Gathelaus.

"Oh no, I'm just telling the grand tale of how I came to be here. Setting it up."

"Do you need your instrument to tell us?"

Brodir smiled. "It wouldn't hurt." Hoskuld handed him the lute and Brodir plucked at it and began. "I didn't know anyone." He paused to tighten a string. "I met the farmer yesterday morning and he said I could ride on the back, same as Hunwulf. He was waiting beside the road as the wagon came by. He had no horse; said he was thrown, and it raced off. He seemed amiable enough and I only spoke to him for the last few miles. I heard you were here and we both spoke of being a part of your revolution and helping you win back the crown from the tyrant Vikarskeid."

"Who brought up my name first?" asked Gathelaus, handing Brodir a bottle of ale.

Brodir drank deeply, then said, "I'm not sure, I might have, he might have, but it came up early as he said something about you and then I think I said I'd serve you if I could find you and he proclaimed that was his mission as well."

Gathelaus grimaced at the tale but Brodir continued, "Men see how the world is turning and seek after a good man to lead them in the fight against the darkness, a king that will lead from the front, take the fight to the enemy and not turn tail. You are that king."

Gathelaus shook his head. "Maybe I was just in the wrong place at the wrong time. Before the first revolution against Forlock, it seemed everyone in Vjorn was ready to accept their lot in life."

"Mountains move when a strong enough man tells them to, that is how people are, when that initial landslide starts down the mountain it is because one man started that rock rolling."

"You use a destructive analogy," remarked Gathelaus.

Brodir strained to sit up from his bed. His excitement caused fresh red to show at his bandages. "Sometimes the old order must be torn down."

"I want change, but I don't want to rebuild the wheel, that isn't my goal, so if you think..."

"No, my king, no. Don't misunderstand me. I only mean that our eyes have been opened and a great many of us see that we cannot live under the oppressive yoke that has been handed us. You helped us all see that. We've all heard what you did singlehandedly for Aldreth. I've been working on a song about that." He strummed the lute. "A lone and brutal man, killing them with kindness, he said time to take back this lan', and with a silver sword take away their blindness."

Gathelaus held a hand to pause the skald. "I was alerted by a good citizen of the realm who had had enough. I didn't even know that mining town existed before the letter."

"But you acted as all good men must. Whatever the cost. And now you are here ridding a lonely, out of the way hamlet of a bloodthirsty dragon. I doubt Vikarskeid has even read the letters Hoskuld has sent."

Gathelaus couldn't argue.

"You are a man for the people to follow."

"My thanks Skald, but it will take more than noble words and platitudes to win against my enemies."

"You have to start somewhere."

"True enough. You get healed. The dragon should come tonight. If I don't succeed, you'll have to find a new focus."

Hoskuld slapped Brodir on the foot and followed Gathelaus out of the chamber. Outside they looked to the sky. Clouds rolled high on the breeze at an incredible pace. "We'll get snow soon."

Gathelaus grunted.

The barmaid from Bjornsburg approached them. Gathelaus meant to thank her for warning him against Hunwulf's treacherous attack, but she spoke first, "Father," she said warmly.

Hoskuld frowned, saying, "Gathelaus, this is my daughter Dahlia. She has unwisely chosen to refuse my counsel to remain in a safe place until Fiendal is dealt with."

The corners of Dahlia's mouth moved ever so slightly from a smile to frown. "I was done hiding; besides, I knew who the huntsmen were following, and I wanted to see what the usurper king would do about it."

"My thanks, good lady, for warning me of Hunwulf's treachery."

"Of course. I wish I had been able to warn you and your comrade sooner back in Bjornsburg. I was pleased you were both able to escape unscathed. You both were able to escape, weren't you?"

"Yes. I have sent my friend Niels on to Hellainik to gather loyal men to assist me."

"Niels? I thought his name was Cap?"

Gathelaus grinned. "He was trying to be discreet. He is a captain of my guard."

She nodded. "And you are here to await the dragon?"

"He has been preparing the last two days to slay Fiendal, if he can," said Hoskuld coldly. "But *you* should not have come back until it is dealt with."

"My place is here," she snapped.

Gathelaus didn't like being between the warring father and daughter so he made an excuse to leave. "I had better go check some of my traps." He took a long step away.

"You know Fiendal is too smart for traps," said Hoskuld.

"I need to know," Dahlia matched Gathelaus's retreat, "what brought you here?"

Gathelaus didn't like where this was going.

Hoskuld cautioned, "Dahlia don't, he is here, that's all that matters."

"What brought you here usurper king?"

"Pure chance," answered Gathelaus.

"I don't think you believe in coincidence any more than I do."

Gathelaus wrinkled his brow. "Are we talking about the same thing?"

"I prayed to Votan to send you here. A mighty man who could slay a dragon," she said.

"No, I was sailing direct to Hellainik, but a storm swamped our craft and we were forced to land in Bjornsburg. Coming past Finnsburg was the fastest way to continue on."

"Then it seems my prayers are more assuredly answered than your own," she said.

Gathelaus snorted. He did pray to Votan on occasion, but it always felt like there was a great divide between himself and the gods, as if any communion between himself and them was beyond reach. He wasn't sure he could trust those that claimed they had that communication.

Hoskuld explained, "She is quite emphatic over the old ways, her mother was a priestess of Votan and Celene. She is walking in those same footsteps."

"But you have chosen to stay?" she asked, looking expectant.

"Yes."

"Because Votan answered my prayer." She smiled at her father.

Gathelaus shrugged. "If you want to see it that way."

She frowned deeper. "Of course, he did. You are here."

"Dahlia is a bit of a zealot," explained Hoskuld. "She sees the gods moving in everything."

"Sounds like that old Pict." Gathelaus nodded curtly and walked away.

"I don't follow Pictish gods," Dahlia called after him. "But even you should acknowledge their divine presence in our lives."

"Never said I didn't," he answered over his shoulder. "But I also do what I want to do regardless of the dogma."

"Dogma?" She stamped her foot, then trotted after him.

He held his hands out, palms toward her. "I do what is right because it is the right thing to do. I can't let a dragon terrorize and murder the innocent."

"Because you would be our king and protector?" Dahlia asked.

"Because I am a man." He turned about and stalked away.

13. DRUM AND FANG

Night fell black as coal and ten times as hard. The last of the wall wardens threw a few cords of wood beside what was now Gathelaus's bonfire, then they too disappeared to whatever shelter they could find for the night. Only the kid and Curu-Calacht remained beside the swordsman.

Hoskuld made a brief appearance. "I'm offering my sincere thanks, Gathelaus. If you can take care of this, I'll be forever in your debt."

"I know," Gathelaus said, tossing a log on the fire. "How about a drink?"

"I'll fetch you some wine." Hoskuld nodded and went back inside the manor house.

After waiting several minutes, he finally heard the bolt slam down and shook his head. "I guess they decided no point in wasting wine on a dead man."

Curu-Calacht chuckled. "That's too bad. I wanted some too, and I have no intention of dying."

"Well, you two can get some sleep or whatever you want. Sure, don't have to stay by me."

The boy nodded to Gathelaus but pointed at a barrel beside the manor house. "I'll be in there."

"Why not? It'll give you a good view."

"I am with you, Gathelaus," said Curu-Calacht. "My magic will help in the fight to come. It will be like in the old times."

Gathelaus liked that, and said, "I'd rather not wait all night. Anything we can do to get Fiendal to come sooner than later?"

The old man produced a skin kettle drum from his deerskin bag. "Fiendal does not like the noise you white men make when celebrating. So, I brought this to help provoke him. This drum will annoy and draw him near in anger. And in anger you can perhaps defeat him as he shall make mistakes, for he is clever, but anger clouds the mind of all creatures it touches."

Gathelaus said, "I'll take you at your word for that." He sat on a stump facing out and away from the fire so he wouldn't be night-blind. He prepared his swords and knives, even the stoutest hammer he could find as well as some rope that he coiled, hoping to use it as a trip-hazard for the behemoth. One end was already tied about the cornerstone of the ruined palace, being the heaviest, most stout object, he could find.

Curu-Calacht sat in the dirt before the fire, heedless of the danger that would surely creep up from behind.

The boy sat slumped over the rim of the barrel, with a dirty blanket across his shoulders. He crunched into an apple and Gathelaus signaled that he wanted one too. The boy, however, wouldn't leave his barrel and threw the apple to Gathelaus, who narrowly caught it before it landed in the roaring fire.

Curu-Calacht began drumming and chanting a song of his people, an old song that called out in the night, noble and fierce. His voice was clear and proud, timed to the steady throb of the drum, calling out the dragon, Fiendal.

"Waiting is always the hard part," Gathelaus lamented to himself. "But being hungry makes the food taste that much better."

The drum's beats echoed and they were answered. An awful roar like angry, cracking thunder swung out of the night and made the few dogs left yip and bark in fear.

Curu-Calacht continued his steady primal beat. To Gathelaus it matched his heart. Upon hearing the terrible roar his heart thumped, *boom, boom, boom, boom*, fast as it could.

The dragon, Fiendal was coming.

Gathelaus felt the big knife at his side; the sharp blade gave him cold comfort. He watched the clouds clearing out as the storm moved on to the south east. The bleak stars appeared and twinkled. They seemed unfeeling and cold, their light frail against the mythic dark.

Curu-Calacht never relaxed and perhaps even drummed a half-beat faster.

Gathelaus stared at the open range toward the cleft, though he could only see a hundred yards at best. A cat or raccoon stole through the edge of the fence line. A night hawk swooped low, briefly illuminated by the firelight. The smell of the pines off the mountain was stronger now after the rain, and the light tremble of every fourth beat rocked Gathelaus upon his stump. Every fourth beat was stronger, shaking the ground harder.

Every fourth beat?

The boy screamed.

Gathelaus swung around to see colossal darkness looming behind. It blocked the stars from view and coalesced into a twelve-foot, mottled grey, tooth ridden horror.

Jaws agape, its massive head tilted slightly as it snapped at Gathelaus who narrowly dodged and rolled away.

On his feet, Gathelaus drew two sturdy Kathulian blades and slashed them into the monster's underbelly as it passed over him. The blades rebounded off the scaly hide. The monster hardly acknowledged the attack at all, giving its lightest roar yet.

Gathelaus rolled again as the swampy tail thrashed where he had just lain. The heavy stump Gathelaus had been sitting on sailed across the yard like a skipping stone.

Grabbing a bow he had set aside earlier, Gathelaus loosed an arrow at the monster's eye or failing that, a nostril. But the behemoth swung around with such speed, Gathelaus's missile was a glancing mark to the monster's impervious jaw line.

The dragon swiftly turned and snapped at him. The hot fetid breath blasting Gathelaus in the face. It smelt of rank death and carrion.

FURY \ \ \ JAMES ALDERDICE

Gathelaus moved swiftly, yet the great taloned feet of Fiendal slammed down and it tore the bow from his grasp. With a crack of wood and twisted steel, the monster's step destroyed the bow.

Racing around the corner of a collapsed wall, Gathelaus hoped for a moment to catch his breath. No such luck.

The heavy step crashed behind him. The dragon spotted him and came on all the swifter. The snapping of the titanic maw gave such fear as Gathelaus had ever known. He weaved as he ran back around the other side of the courtyard and dropped near a water trough for cover. Gathelaus had applied sulphur here earlier to mask his scent.

The drumming, if not the chant of Curu-Calacht, continued, and Gathelaus reeled at the thought of the old man still singing what could only be his death song.

Was it a distraction? The monster nudged at the trough as if to coax Gathelaus into revealing himself to be run down and eaten. But the drumming worked. The monster, having lost both the scent and sight of Gathelaus, wheeled to go after Curu-Calacht.

Fiendal cleared half the distance as Gathelaus rose to attempt his other trap. He raced forward and took hold of the rope he had concealed in the dust and debris on the ground. Gripping it as tight as he could he looped it round a broken pillar and made ready to pull it tight. In so doing this maneuverer he had revealed himself to the dragon's peripheral vision, however.

Curu-Calacht drummed and chanted louder without fear.

The monster hesitated to look at both men. Curu-Calacht retreated a few paces, still banging the drum and giving his loud throaty chant.

Fiendal paused, taking in the location of Gathelaus and the drumming man in front of it. It roared once more and took a step toward Curu-Calacht, the line catching at its ankles as Gathelaus pulled it tight. The dragon stepped and the line pulled hard. Gathelaus braced himself to hang on, hoping like hell the monster would fall on its face, where he might be able to rush it and stab his sword into its eye.

Gathelaus attempted to hold the line, cursing at the loss of the bow.

Curu-Calacht pounded the drum and took another few steps backward, his eyes never leaving that of the dragon before him.

"Come demon and meet your doom!" grated Gathelaus.

Fiendal staggered a moment but kicked out and the pillar the line was wrapped twice around suddenly flew away. Gathelaus was carried with it several paces before letting go and landing with a face full of dirt in his teeth. He sprang up and drew his broadsword, ready to charge at the dragon. Opposite the blazing bonfire, the monster stared at him hungrily… and Curu-Calacht was gone!

They circled each other about the bonfire. Gathelaus stayed around the edge of the circle, trying to keep light on his feet. He was a big brute of a man, yet so much smaller than the monster. He guessed that he was quicker than the massive foe; or at least he hoped he was quicker. If he wasn't, he'd be dead.

Fiendal lunged, champing his massive jaws at Gathelaus, snorting angrily every time the meal escaped its grasp.

Gathelaus kept moving, rolling and ducking out of the way of that spinning tail, crunching feet, and those great black claws which left scars across the flagstones.

The swordsman smote his gleaming blade against the gray skin, but always the edge slipped off as if the dragon's skin was heavy steel plate.

Fiendal retaliated by launching his own attack against Gathelaus. It crunched after the fleeing man, tearing with its feet, and snatched up a scarecrow Gathelaus had positioned as a decoy.

The dragon spit the sticks and straw away, shaking its head as if furious that it had been tricked.

Gathelaus charged, beating his sword against the brute until the tail swung out, pitching him onto his face. He nearly cut himself on his own blade. He rolled away just as Fiendal's huge foot slammed into the ground where he had just been. Sparks shot from the stone.

Curu-Calacht shot arrows at Fiendal, but these skittered off the iron hard skin in futility.

Gathelaus again slammed his blade across the belly of the beast but was knocked aside as the monster hopped forward. He scrambled up just in time to see the mouth reaching, and snapping shut. The smell of the fetid breath was like death blasting him in the face.

Gathelaus slashed his sword across the back side of the great monster's ankle, again there was no result, no blood, no triumph in this bloody tragedy.

Roaring in anger, Fiendal scattering the bonfire with its great tail. Flame and smoke shot across the hall and dark shadows danced like demons in communion, kindling small blazes into existence among the hay and debris of the courtyard.

Knowing Fiendal's skin was thick and scaled overlapping like mail, Gathelaus strove to ram the tip of his sword as hard as he could straight into the monster's belly. All his strength was for naught as the blade hit true but slipped away against the horrible monster's impenetrable skin. His great blade of the finest workmanship was bent at almost a right angle! Shock at this weapon's failure made him pause a deadly second.

Fiendal stepped back to reach the foe, its jaw snapped onto Gathelaus's scale-mail sleeve, tearing the links apart as if they were no stronger than petals in the wind.

He slammed his bent great sword at the monster's face, but the awful muzzle knocked it away. Gathelaus rolled as a terrible foot slammed down and clawed deep furrows into the ground where he had just been. He was unarmed against his greatest foe.

The Kathulian sword had been a gift of the gods. There was no foe he had not slain with it, now it was broken, useless. Why had he been abandoned by the gods? Was he meant to die here and now? Swallowed up by the jaws of this voracious monster? Oh, the fates are cruel.

The words of his father came. *When the sword breaks, you pick up a stone.*

No time for despair, he was a weapon beyond any sword. He would find a way.

"Here Fiendal! Here! See what I have in store for you!" cried Curu-Calacht, shouting for the dragon's attention.

As the monster threatened Curu-Calacht, Gathelaus dropped his useless sword and charged bare handed at the brute. "Votan!" he roared like a madman.

The drum beat louder as Fiendal salivated.

Likely sensing the man running at him, he swept his tail out, swaying like a vertical battering ram.

Dodging away from its attack, Gathelaus scrutinized the monster. It killed with its mouth, with its clawed feet, and with its great sweeping tail, but Fiendal did not use his tiny arms.

"Northman!" cried Curu-Calacht as he cast a spear to Gathelaus.

Gathelaus caught the spear as Fiendal lunged again with his mouth agape. He slammed the point into the roof of the monstrous mouth. Fiendal snapped its jaws shut and the shaft splintered apart in Gathelaus's hands. The spearhead was lost inside, but there was blood running from the monster's mouth, and it was not that of his earlier victims.

"See that! It bleeds! We can kill it!" shouted Gathelaus.

Fiendal roared in maddening pain and spun about with crazed anger flashing in its yellow eyes. Folk emboldened by Gathelaus's cry of triumph watched from behind far corners.

Curu-Calacht took up a sling and sent a stone pelting the dragon on its snout. "Go back to your cave. Leave this place! Your time here is done!"

Fiendal roared at the old Pict and if the spear and stone had made him think of retreating, that small victory was gone. Fiendal charged ahead toward the tall old Pict.

He had one more idea. At the edge of the wall lay a bucket of tarry oil with a long rope attached.

While Fiendal was occupied with Curu-Calacht, Gathelaus took up the rope and swung the weight around and around, until it had terrific momentum.

"Watch out Curu!" he called, as he prayed to Votan that he had timed it right. The bucket went flying and splashed the inky ichor all over Fiendal's snout.

Fiendal's head jerked back and forth at the unpleasant substance, but it was not beaten yet.

Gathelaus snatched up a torch and threw it against the monster's gory head. But he missed and the torch hit the ground at the monster's feet.

Fiendal wheeled like a striking serpent and narrowed its great amber eye at Gathelaus.

FURY 〉〉〉 JAMES ALDERDICE

A bloodcurdling howl sounded and an enormous wolfman hurtled atop Fiendal's head, clawing and slashing.

Gathelaus was astounded, but as the two monstrous combatants snapped at one another, they moved enough that he dared go and retrieve the torch. He reached the still flickering flame and called for Curu-Calacht. "Curu!" He spun about looking for the old Pict, but he was nowhere to be found.

The two monsters tore at one another, Fiendal snapping its jaws, nearly capturing the wolfman as he slid over the top of the dragon's skull.

Gathelaus wondered could the old Pict be the werewolf?

"Throw the torch!" called the wolfman, as he leapt away from the dragon, running down its back, and just avoided the swinging tail.

Gathelaus threw the torch. It struck Fiendal across the snout. Flames leapt to life, igniting the sticky oil.

Fiendal roared, then dove at the ground and rolled to extinguish the blaze. His thrashing so great that his tail battered down a section of the outer wall. What was left of the bonfire was snuffed out and the smoking logs batted far astride. Even the barrel the boy was hiding in was sent rolling away down the courtyard.

Worst of all, the wolfman, or Curu-Calacht, was caught in the maelstrom and crushed beneath the pained monster.

Gathelaus glanced about for another weapon, formulating another plan.

Curu cried out in agony, but Gathelaus could not reach him as the dragon yowled and twisted over the ground. Bricks and battlements were tossed aside like leaves in the hurricane by the power of Fiendal's thrashing. Gathelaus leapt away as another lashing of the monster's tail brought one of the posts holding the rafters of the stable down, making the thatch slump and spill inside the straw covered floor.

Gathelaus hoped that perhaps the monster was blinded or even wounded unto death with the burns, but abruptly the fire was out and Fiendal stood tall again, casting a wary gaze over the courtyard.

Curu-Calacht was a pile of smashed human bones, yet something more.

His limbs looked strangely elongated and covered in coarse grey fur.

Fiendal roared once again and loped out of the courtyard. He was angry but perhaps would think twice about coming into Finnsburg again.

The dragon roared several times more but moved swiftly away. Why he had left when he did Gathelaus could not be sure. He ran to Curu-Calacht's side and marveled at the half-transformed man. His blood leaked out from a hundred different wounds, but it was clear he was not fully human. His shattered body was frozen in mid-transformation.

"I used the last of my magic to send him away, that you might prepare again, and win," said Curu-Calacht with a wretched wheeze.

"You were the guardian in the forest."

"Yes." He paused as he coughed up blood. "But I am the last of my clan and the last guardian of the old ways."

He clutched Gathelaus's hand and held it weakly. All strength had fled from him. "Burn me. It is our way. Do not let the folk of Finnsburg know my great secret and curse my name."

Gathelaus nodded solemnly. "I will."

Curu-Calacht passed with the claws of a wolf but the heart of a man.

Gathelaus covered Curu-Calacht with a blanket so that as folk crept out to see the carnage, they would not see the half-transformed man and judge him harshly. He gathered the scattered wood and started a new burn pile atop the dead Pictish guardian.

The pyre blazed bright as the red finger of dawn rose over the mountain.

14. REMEMBER THE TUNE

With dawn's light, folk took stock of the additional destruction and many complained that Gathelaus's presence had only made things worse. The damage to the stables and entrance to the great hall were terrible.

"He also burned that old Pict's body right in our courtyard," shouted one the men to Hoskuld. "Now that old Pict's specter will haunt our hamlet!"

Hoskuld gave a wary eye to Gathelaus, asking an explanation without words.

"He will not haunt you. He was crushed by the dragon. Funeral pyre is the Pictish way. Besides, the fire will clear away any trace. Don't be so superstitious considering the bloodshed that had already occurred here."

"Aye," argued one of the men, "bloodshed is all that your foul name brings here!"

"Gathelaus the usurper's name equals blood and death!" cried another.

Several more folk cheered both men's comments and vented their frustrations at Gathelaus.

"Regardless of what you think of me, I will finish this dragon," Gathelaus said stubbornly.

Dahlia came forward, shouting, "A man tries to make a difference and you attack him for it?"

"He brings the doom upon us!" called one of the farmers.

"It's amazing he hasn't been eaten already. Knut Hrakkison already told us how Gathelaus hid in Knut's shelter the first night. He is no hero," shouted another.

"He might even be in league with the demon dragon!" screeched an old woman.

Hoskuld held his hands up, demanding silence. "Enough, Gathelaus is my guest and you will not badger him any longer."

Another man stood forward, proclaiming, "Everything has been tried so far but the old ways. We should do a sacrifice to send the dragon away."

The crowd cheered at this notion, though no one had been clear on what that was.

"The old gods demanded blood. The blood of an innocent. Let us give Fiendal innocent blood that this calamity may be over!"

Gathelaus stepped forward. "What you ask has never worked. It is the refuge of a foolish mind. Blood gods will only demand more blood! I have seen this to be true in far off lands."

The crowd cursed at him and hurled more insults.

Hoskuld demanded of the vicious crowd, "And what innocent blood would you sacrifice? My daughter? Your own daughters? This is not how we do things anymore."

Dahlia put a hand on her father's shoulder and said loudly, "I have prayed for a solution and last night in a vison, I beheld a dream of my dear mother, whom you all know, and she told me that this man would find a way to end this dragon and strife in our lands. Do you trust me Knut Hrakkison? Do you Rognor? And you Gil Hrut? Do you trust my visons?"

The angry folk eased back at their favored daughter. Fearful and frustrated as they were, they would not gainsay her.

"We trust your dreams dear Dahlia; your mother was a favored woman. But hunger makes us speak unkind words and fear retribution beyond what we can bear."

Dahlia shouted, "I know all these things, and it is why I have come back. I also know that Gathelaus, the former king, is our champion. When he is done with the dragon, I am sure he will send for assistance, as he knows our terrible plight."

Hoskuld approached his daughter smiling wide and took her in his arms proudly. "My good daughter speaks true. We stand together and will overcome this evil!"

The crowd cheered and the fire of their anger was cooled.

When he had the opportunity, Gathelaus asked Dahlia, softly, "Did you have such a vision?"

"No," she whispered, "but I want to believe it. So, I am asking you to make it come true. All of it."

He gave her a curt bow, saying, "Flesh and blood could no more resist your words than a blade."

FURY ✝ ✝ ✝ JAMES ALDERDICE
✝ ✝ ✝

After the coals had cooled on Curu-Calacht's pyre, Gathelaus carefully gathered the bones, put them in a sack, and carried them off into the woods not far beyond the shrine to Votan. There he made a small cairn and bid his own respects to the forest shaman.

He finished at midafternoon and then heard horsemen coming down the road. He stepped carefully through the trees, remaining unseen as he watched to see who they were. Upon recognizing Niels and other comrades in arms, he stepped out and raised a hand in salute.

With Niels were just under a dozen riders. Some of them he recognized from his old guard and company. Men he had not seen in well over a year now. "Hail Niels and old friends, I am glad to see you."

"And we you, oh king," said Thorne, riding up beside Gathelaus and dismounting. They clasped hands like long lost brothers, and then embraced. "So what next? Niels said a dragon plagues this land?"

"It does. I mean to slay it and from there take the fight back to Vikarskeid."

Thorne nodded. "It has been hard in your absence. Many of the old company have left the countryside, for Vikarskeid hunts all of us down at every turn. Seems he has spies that swore you still lived, and so that gave us hope yet."

"I thank you for your loyalty."

"Friendship is beyond loyalty," said Thorne.

Gathelaus said, "This way, I'll show you to the hall and we'll make a plan for the dragon."

Niels asked, "What were you doing with that cairn? Anything I should know?"

"The wolfshead," said Gathelaus.

Niels' eyes went wide, but no more words were said.

"But I have another surprise for you, Niels, so try to keep your tongue behind your teeth when you see it."

Niels gave a questioning look. "What did I say?"

Thorne laughed and clapped him hard on the back.

They walked or rode back inside the walls to the courtyard, and Gathelaus said to Hoskuld, who was speaking with Bors near the gatehouse, "Lord Hoskuld. These are my men and will assist me as much as they can with the dragon. We will not be a bother to you as far as your food stores go, but we will need ale for the men and grain for the horses."

"Welcome friends of Gathelaus," said Hoskuld. "I'm a poor host but will do what I can."

Dahlia came from inside the hall and Niels' eyes gaped. He glanced at Gathelaus.

"Lord Hoskuld's daughter," said Gathelaus. "Her name is Dahlia."

"I know," said Niels, taking off his hat.

FURY ↯ ↯ ↯ JAMES ALDERDICE

"Hello, Cap," she said, with a mischievous grin.

"Yes, well, it's actually Captain Niels," he said, blushing a little.

"You're turning red, Cap," said Thorne, giving Niels a friendly shove.

"I'll let you all get settled," said Gathelaus, "I want to speak with the skald about something else that I've been wondering."

Niels stared at Dahlia, likely missing every word Gathelaus had said. Thorne chuckled and shook hands with Hoskuld.

↯ ↯ ↯

Gathelaus went to the root cellar that had been turned into the skald's recovery room. As he went down the steps, he heard Brodir singing and strumming his lute. "My lady's eyes are dark and wet, for she knows, that when it snows, that she can bet, that I'll be getting on down the road, nude but all covered in woad, and so she'll miss my kisses all the more."

Sari joined him in the chorus, "Down the road, all covered in woad, a Pict for a friend and a sword in the end, and I'll be missing his kissing all the more."

The lute playing abruptly stopped as Sari launched herself atop Brodir and while he gladly welcomed the embrace, he cried out in pain of his wound.

"I'm so sorry," she gasped.

"It's all right," wheezed Brodir, with a pained expression. "Some sacrifices are worthwhile."

Gathelaus coughed. "Am I interrupting anything?"

Sari leapt back, acting as if she hadn't just been trying to smother Brodir with kisses. "I'd better see to your bandages," she said keeping up the charade, though her hair was a mess.

"Not at all," said Brodir. "I was just letting Sari, here, know what to do if she happens to get bit by a poisonous snake. Same thing as a mermaid as it turns out."

"Mermaids don't bite," said Sari.

Brodir kicked off his blanket, proclaiming, "Look at my calf, girl, and tell me they don't." There was a peculiar scar there, though it looked more like a horse bite to Gathelaus.

"Oh, dear," gasped Sari. "How did you ever suck out the poison by yourself?"

Brodir said sternly, "Always have help with that one, my love." Then he winked. She blushed.

"I had better go see about your dinner." She left the room swaying and giddy, as if she were ten years younger.

"You picked a fine time to come calling, my king," said Brodir, not more than a little annoyed.

"I think you'll recover all the same."

"Well, what can I do for you?"

Gathelaus said, "I have been wondering what more I can learn about the dragon."

"I have yet to see the monster myself," said Brodir. "Though I have heard near the same tales as you, I'm sure, but I doubt the folk have told me anything you haven't witnessed yourself already."

Gathelaus went on. "Too right, but I wonder about older knowledge that has been preserved, not in books or scrolls, or even memory of man, but in song."

"Song? Ah, I think I catch your meaning."

Gathelaus asked Brodir, "Do you know the old song about the wyrm of Finnsburg?"

"Yea, that old one about a Sigurd who slew a dragon here?"

"That's the one."

Brodir said, "Soon as my fingers remember the tune, my tongue will too." He strummed a moment on his lute, tuning the instrument. His fingers ran over the fret board as he warmed to the strings. *"Sigurd was a king, with an iron hand. Wait, that's not right, hold on."*

"A king is a man, who rules by his own hand
But t'was heroes like Sigurd who tamed this land
Whether raider, slayer, or dark deceiver came
They met their end on his blade just the same
With bandits and beasts, he did collide
Giving all of them that final steel ride
Across the mountains and plains, his black company rode
And here, he heard of that great long-tailed toad
For Fiendal the dragon was about and hungered he for blood

FURY \ \ \ JAMES ALDERDICE

The death he wrought covered the land like a flood
Now the sword, spear and axe did brave Sigurd wield
But none of them could break through the dragon shield
Steel made by man is what he intended on Fiendal to feed
Though it was broken bones that made the dragon bleed
For no weapon forged by man could strike the deadly blow
It was a blade crafted by a wolf witch don't you know
Halla made a broad double-bladed axe of silver and gold
A wise smith, she covered it with runes ancient and cold
With this weapon in hand alone, did Sigurd knock free
And steal from the dragon teeth numbered but three
Back to his mother and the marsh and back to his lair
Did Fiendal run away and to this day stay there."

Gathelaus listened well and pondered. "Thank you, Brodir."

Brodir strummed the lute again a time or two, racing his fingers across the frets. "I think I remembered it all right, though I could give it a better try once I'm healed."

"No, that was more than enough. I was seeking insight into the old ways of dealing with the dragon. I hoped that song might preserve something, and it did."

Brodir wrinkled his brow. "Sometimes a song is just a song. I've never heard one that talked about treasure that was still where the song said it was. By the time I sing about it, our grandfathers, grandfather has already gone digging and found only an empty hole."

"Right, but knowledge or even legend on how a dragon was defeated isn't going to change."

Brodir raised a finger and tapped his temple saying, "So you need a wolf witch who can make a magic axe?"

"Maybe, but the song said more than that."

"So you don't need a wolf witch then?" He arched a single brow questioningly, as he gave a quick strum on the lute.

"I think we might have an easier time finding the axe these days," said Gathelaus.

"True," said Brodir. "Though finding it now doesn't seem terribly likely to me."

Gathelaus shrugged. "I might have disbelieved a short time ago, but these days I have seen things that make me rethink my superstitions and doubts."

Brodir nodded sagely. "Then I shall endeavor to help you find that axe."

"My thanks. I'll prepare to fight the dragon again. I have a new plan of attack now. I should have listened to Curu-Calacht the first time."

"Who, the old Pict?"

Gathelaus nodded. "I know what I need to do."

"I hope its more than a last throw of the dice," said Brodir.

"No substitute for victory," Gathelaus answered.

15. ARMED TO THE TEETH

"Will it work?" asked the Dahlia. "They say Fiendal has slain a ship full of warriors."

"My Lord has never failed in slaying monsters," answered Brodir the skald. He was confined to sitting at a bench because of his wound, but none of that had slowed his gregarious nature.

"There is always a first time," said Dahlia with a nervous smile. She regretted any possible insult to Gathelaus.

"Then I pray to Votan that I get to witness it," laughed the Skald, before quaffing a tankard of foaming ale and slamming it down on a table. He grabbed one of the serving wenches about the waist, forcing a kiss upon her full lips before she half-heartedly escaped his tenuous hold.

Dahlia was a curious witness to this brazen spectacle and had kept to herself in the shadows, while the warriors pledged to Gathelaus worked furiously within the great hall, clearing out tables and benches. Her father had forbidden her from being a part of this, but she had avoided his sight and remained forever nearby the preparations.

The men pushed most of the furnishings off to the side, stacking them. A great bonfire blazed in the center of the hall, smoke erupting up to the rafters and out the wagon-sized hole above. Stars were visible through the curling smoke, watching like the unblinking eyes of the old gods themselves.

"Will you care to join us?" asked the Skald. "I have a kettle drum, tambourine, or a harp for you to make noise with." He shook the tambourine in her direction and tossed it to her.

She caught it. "Seems a strange way to attract a hungry monster."

The Skald laughed, saying, "I can't think of a better way to lure the dragon in. They say he hates joyous music."

Dahlia grinned to herself, for the drunken Skald's idea of communal music was painful and discordant. "I hope you're right."

The warriors each banged the drum or strummed their various strings, none of which was particularly soothing or joyous, but it was very loud.

"You will be staying?" asked Niels, as he patted a small drum.

"I suppose I will for a time. I don't want to be in the way, but I want to see the dragon fall."

Niels stepped closer, patting the drum. It sounded like a heartbeat and she had no doubt at all that his beat for her. "I'll keep you safe."

"But if my father sees me, I'll get quite the scolding. And you can't protect me from his ire," she said with a smile.

"Then we best slay that dragon soon," said Niels, thumping the drum louder.

Dahlia looked to the center of the hall and saw Gathelaus unstrapping his scale mail. He took off his shirt and tunic, then secured his sword belt. He was readying himself for the confrontation. She strode up to Gathelaus asking, "Are you ready?"

"Aye," he answered. "Done this before I can do it again."

"Will he come?"

"Of course," said Gathelaus with a laugh.

"Is it every other night?"

"Lord Hoskuld certainly thinks so."

Dahlia looked over the hall. These men didn't look like they were expecting a dragon to arrive. It looked like drunken madness, a celebration when everyone should be running for their lives. "It's almost like everyone here wants to die. You already said you couldn't hurt it."

Gathelaus snorted. "I did hurt it a little, but now I know what I must do."

The discordant barrage of drums and strings blared into the night.

Dahlia said, "Are you sure you haven't let the legend of your own mind win control? Some things a man can't do."

"Niels, if you want to see to the safety of the women such as Lady Dahlia, you have my leave," said Gathelaus, knowing full well that would shame Niels into action.

Niels banged the drum all the louder, shouting, "Not I, my lord. I know you set a high standard for the protection of the innocent, but I must be present."

Dahlia said, "I meant no disrespect, but the monster Fiendal is old as time. He has slain all the other heroes who have faced him yet."

"A hero does, what he must," Gathelaus answered. "And I do it because it is the right thing to do. I would not see anyone left to be the meal of a monster. It is the right thing to do."

"He's lying," cried Brodir the Skald. "He wants the glory of being the slayer of all monsters!"

Gathelaus clapped the Skald across the shoulders and shoved him. "He speaks the truth. I do want to have the sagas mention my name long after I am gone."

Niels raised a toast of his honey mead at that response. Dahlia did the same, though now, she almost feared her father's presence more than the monster.

"Have at it! Everyone play louder," cried Gathelaus. Tinkling cymbals and sounding brass echoed from the hall. "They say the beast hates music and laughter!"

"Just like my last wife," shouted the Skald. The Northmen laughed.

"They say no weapon can harm him, that its skin is like iron," reminded Dahlia.

Gathelaus drank from his tankard, finished it, then nodded while he wiped away the froth clinging to his stubbled beard. "I have heard that tale from near everyone. But I've never seen anything that couldn't be slain one way or another."

"Demons? Djinn? Ghosts?" questioned the Dahlia. "Surely there must have been something you couldn't kill, and I would hate for tonight to be a surprise."

Gathelaus drew his sword. The mottled grey steel caught the firelight in strange patterns across its edge. "Blessed weapons have won the day against all foes thus far."

Dahlia humbly agreed, yet fearful of what could be done against supernatural opponents. She knew he had seen strange things in his far travels and yet no one had ever claimed they could harm a ghost or demon before Gathelaus had.

"Are you ready for this? No one standing has brought weapons to bear against Fiendal and remained unscathed."

"I am ready," said Gathelaus. Directing his fingers around the handle of his sword, he felt the scored lines. The grip was solid and would not slip, even if it was covered in blood, which it had been many times. He swung the blade up and over his shoulders, stretching his muscles and reminding himself of that deadly dance. "Walk with me," he said to Dahlia. Niels followed.

They strode to the front door of the hall, pushed it aside and stepped out into the cold air. The wind hit them full in the face like the storm god, Votan's thrown hammer. It stole Dahlia's breath for a moment. The light frosted snow outside crunched beneath their boots. Moonlight reached out and cast a frozen gleam on their floating breath. Behind them, the music crashed like shield-walls in battle.

Somewhere on that bleak horizon, the monster heard and gave a cry of anger.

"That's what I wanted to hear," said Gathelaus. "Fiendal is coming."

"You smile to hear death? What if you fail? What will become of your men, your family, your very soul?"

"If a man can't smile at death, then what is he doing with his life?" answered Gathelaus.

"But your family! Your children would be fatherless."

"I would have the songs of my deeds lull my children to sleep. Worry profits a man nothing, but tales of courage gives him all the hope he will ever need. Why do you think I keep the skald around?"

Dahlia considered Gathelaus's words once again, she wondered if he made a mistake having those men here. But if men can't follow their lord into the devil's mouth, they couldn't follow anyone with any faith. Gathelaus didn't look left or right as he pushed past the bearded faces but kept his steely gaze straight ahead. He felt the men closing in behind, heard them set their shields around the edge of the hall. They were ready and he was clearly proud of them. The folk of Hoskuld, on the other hand, whispered to each other, she heard their trepidation, their fear, their excitement.

"Let's get to it," Gathelaus said. "Bar the door."

Dahlia thought about that and the reckless manner all these warriors possessed. They all smiled at the death that was coming for them. But then it comes for all men, so shouldn't they smile and enjoy the time they have and relish the joy of battle and brotherhood alike?

They went back inside, and the men barred the door with an old plank. They wanted Fiendal to think it was closed but not unassailable. Then they gathered their shields, swords and axes and lined up along the inside, ready to defend themselves if the beast got past their lord.

"You best stay close to your nook, or your father would never forgive me," said Gathelaus.

"I'll keep an eye on her," said Niels.

"Not more than you watch my back, I should hope," teased Gathelaus.

Somewhere out in the cold distance the monster roared again, the echoes died down and pushed back, then silence remained like a black tide.

They didn't have long to wait as something growled outside. The horses shrieked in terrible fear then bolted away from the stables.

Heavy steps thundered outside the hall. Snorting breath blasted in through an open window, though nothing could yet be seen. The window was as high as two men standing atop each other. Steps rounded the hall twice until something slammed up against the doors, cracking the bar in one fell push.

Gathelaus stood facing the doors, his back to the fire, and he seemed a god himself. Perhaps a crazed god of fire and war, but a deity, nonetheless.

FURY ⚔ ⚔ ⚔ JAMES ALDERDICE

The doors flung open and wind pushed in like a phalanx of invisible demons. A great, black shape formed as the doors fell away. It stood upright like a man, but it was taller, filling the grand doorway all the way to the etched keystone. Its taloned footsteps struck the flagstones like hammers against an anvil.

A strange kind of fear tugged at Dahlia, but she could not look away from the terrible monster. It was a mindless panic like being trapped beneath the ice. She forced herself not to look away, to face down this devil. She would support these new sword brothers who had come to defend her homeland.

Dahlia was struck at how tiny the monster's arms were. It was as her father had said. It killed with its mouth or feet; the arms were virtually useless. For as large as Fiendal was, the arms were no bigger than Gathelaus's own.

Fiendal was a giant, with scaly, ash-gray skin and leering, yellow eyes. Its great snout had massive teeth jutting out that were as big as a man's hand. Drool fell from its mouth like a spilled tankard of ale. Its arms were small, no bigger than a man's, but its feet were like tree trunks and its sweeping tail, the same as a leviathan's and big as a cedar. It strode into the hall, stooping against the foremost rafters. A few of the wall wardens struck at its dragging tail but it swept out and knocked them asunder.

A few of Gathelaus's shield men attacked but fell away as the monster swung about attempting to crush them under its taloned feet.

FURY ⚔ ⚔ ⚔ JAMES ALDERDICE

Gathelaus stepped forward. Dahlia guessed that it was a hard step to take, as if he was pushing against a great river of doubt, but he took that step anyway, tilted his head back, and looked Fiendal full in the face, shouting, "I'm Gathelaus, rightful king of Vjorn, and I'll suffer no monster to live."

Fiendal stared at him, tongue lolling. It roared once like the rolling of thunder upon the wind-tossed sea.

⚔ ⚔ ⚔

Gathelaus roared back with all the fury of the north. The men surrounding in the hall roared their zeal for this confrontation. They charged in and slashed away at the armored skin. Blades were bent, and none drew blood, but there was courage in numbers and zeal in their assault.

Fiendal blinked, taking note of the men encircled about him like a barricade. This wasn't like last time, it must have thought.

It lashed again with its tail and sent Gathelaus flying back against the wall, the sword tossed from his grip. Fiendal stepped upon the blade and snapped the steel.

In the crackling gleam of the retreating firelight, Fiendal's attention swept over burning logs, the wailing of the dying, and the envigored cries of the fighting shield-wall. It roared back contemptuously.

"We've accomplished nothing yet, lads! He'll eat our bones for the insult of that mere pinprick of pain we caused him if we don't kill him now!"

The men of the shield-wall roared back at Fiendal from all sides. It slathered its tongue at them, running it along the jagged edges of its oversized teeth. Thunder in his belly boomed that he would sup well tonight.

Fiendal roared and snapped at a pikeman, who managed to get the edge caught in the dragons' teeth. He was picked up and tossed across the hall to move no more.

The killer instinct within Gathelaus awoke. The red ballad of death sang and Gathelaus knew the tune. Whether it was helped along by the great invisible spirit as Curu-Calacht had said, it mattered not, because the man in his struggle against death answered the call.

Gathelaus seized the chaotic moment, ran, and leapt up the monster's bent knee. He grabbed hold of the monster's right arm and held on for the ride of his life.

The monster turned with snapping jaws, reaching for Gathelaus, but could not get close enough to bite the irritating man. Its deadly taloned feet strained but couldn't reach up to claw away its foe, nor could its tail slap Gathelaus away. The arms, each with but two clawed fingers, were especially useless, and strain as it might, it could not reach Gathelaus with its tenacious grip. The monster swung about looking to jerk its enemy free, but he would not let go. Fiendal screamed in protest.

Gathelaus was flung into the air a time or two, but he held onto the scaly arm like cold to ice. Fiendal tired and slowed a moment. Using all his strength, Gathelaus twisted the arm backward as far as it would go.

The monster swung its massive body in circles in a panic, as if possibly hoping to toss or shake the man aside like a dog scratching fleas.

Gathelaus hung on for dear life as he was dizzied by the spinning monster. Like the bull of the gods, Gathelaus rode the dragon, shouting, "Votan!"

That prayer to the storm god on his smashed and bloody lips, Gathelaus reached deep inside for more strength and pulled until he felt the bone jog loose within cartilage. Gathelaus swung back and, taking hold at the monster's elbow, slammed it backward until the shoulder bone snapped.

Fiendal screamed.

"Votan!" cried Gathelaus.

Fiendal's eyes rolled up in shock. It squawked like a chick for its mother.

Gathelaus knew now that Fiendal had never felt pain like this, had never known fear like this. He was hurting this monstrous fiend!

Fiendal jerked and twisted, snorting till blood foamed pink at his nostrils, and still the bear of a man would not let go.

For the first time ever, Fiendal knew fear. This man, this insect, was hurting it. It snapped at the man but could not even come close to grasping the tenacious foe.

Gathelaus took the broken arm, twisting it like rope, turning and bending it back and forth until a piece of the jagged bone beneath sheared through the mottled gray skin. Fiendal spun about like a whirlwind, slamming into the gilded posts within the hall, crying like all the devils in hell.

Hot blood ran down Fiendal's arm drenching Gathelaus in crimson gore. This was glorious butchery. This was payback.

Fiendal screamed again and vomited in terror.

One last twist and pull.

The arm came loose and Gathelaus fell to the ground, still clutching the scaly arm and two finger-like claws.

Fiendal roared, eyes rolling in pain, then leaned down and snapped at Gathelaus.

Gathelaus answered him back by battering the dragon across the snout with its own severed arm.

Blood spurted in gouts across the flagstones. Fiendal screamed and retreated toward the gates of the hall.

The sword company held their shields, trying to block its escape. Gathelaus was coming, painted red with Fiendal's blood, and holding the arm aloft like a grim trophy.

Fiendal charged at the shield-wall and plowed them asunder like liar's dice. It was plain he feared the man with his stolen arm more than anything it could have conceived before this night. It had been king of all it surveyed, it had ruled the swamps of dragons and monsters. Now, it had been brow-beaten with one of its own body parts. It fled, barking sick fear into the night, back into the howling winds and snows.

Deep scarlet splashed across Gathelaus's face as Fiendal ran into the darkness, bawling more like a crippled goat than the thunder lizard it was.

Gathelaus held the bloody clawed arm aloft and shouted the barbaric cry of victory. This time it was his voice that rocked the night and made the beasts fall silent.

The bloodied Niels was among those that still stood. He looked to Gathelaus. "Now what?"

"We pursue and destroy him. See, he leaves a steaming blood trail even a civilized city-born man like you could follow." Gathelaus, slapped Niels hard on the back. "Let's go! We'll have slain a dragon by morning!"

16. TO THE MARSH

With the terrible bawling retreat of Fiendal, the folk of Finnsburg stepped out from their shadows and hiding places.

Hoskuld came out marveling at the gory sight of Fiendal's defeat. "I never would have believed," he muttered time and again, staring at the arm in Gathelaus's hand.

"Get my horse," ordered Gathelaus. "Fiendal's got a blood trail flowing like the Rites River. We need to finish this tonight."

"You heard the man," shouted Hoskuld. "Gather the horses!"

One of the wall wardens handed the reins of a horse to Gathelaus and he traded him Fiendal's sundered arm. The man almost dropped the arm he was so astounded. Gathelaus mounted and rode out of the gates in pursuit, followed by the men as swiftly as they could reach a horse.

The wall warden held up Fiendal's terrible clawed arm and waved it about like a trophy.

Dahlia came out from where she had been sheltered. She saw the men mounting their horses to pursue Fiendal. She saw the torn arm. "He did it!"

Hoskuld was assisted by Bors in mounting his horse. "He did. But you stay here and wait."

"No, I am coming. I want to see the dragon's death."

"No!" shouted Hoskuld. "It's heading back to the marsh where more of its verminous brethren may be. You stay here!" He rode past her.

She glanced back at the arm the old wall warden still held. Already a crowd of folk pressed in to see and touch the gory relic. She ran to find a horse for herself and follow.

A dozen men rode into the darkness after the monster, following the blood trail across the snowy meadows and through the quaking aspens. Gory amounts of red were splashed across the ground in great spurts almost every seven paces, the stride of the great dragon and the timing of its mighty heart blasting out blood onto the cold ground.

As they neared the marsh, steam yet rose from the pool of hot blood, and some of the men slowed their pace, now unsure if they still wished to find the dragon breathing.

Through the tall thick grasses and all the way to the marsh, the blood painted a trail to follow. Even upon the inky waters, crimson swirled toward the cleft in the rock. And there upon a swampy inlet, Fiendal had collapsed, having gone as close to its home as it could manage.

"Maybe we should wait till the break of day," suggested Bors. "No telling what might be in the water waiting for us. I've heard tales of great flesh-eating eels."

Gathelaus's eyes flashed savagely, the hunters instinct on him too strong to wait, too strong to let things go. It was too strong to deny. "Wait here if you like, I'm going to finish him."

He stalked into the reeds and waters alone until he stepped in a hole and almost had to swim. He trudged out of the cool waters and upon the stony rise. The only sound was the waterfall against the cliff face. The blood trail beckoned him on into the darkness of the fissure like the promise of a cooing lover. The waterfall beside him that fed the marsh cast a deafening dull roar.

Behind him, he saw some of the men slowly following, moving sluggishly forward through the reeds.

The cleft wound through a copse of reeds and finally into a sheltering overhang of rock where the bones of monstrous generations rotted and the supposed last of its kind came to die.

Fiendal lay upon its belly, snorting blood in clotted pools before its great nostrils as it breathed heavily. Its massive amber eyes blinked slowly. The wound of its stolen arm spurted jets of blood in time with its dying heartbeat. Gathelaus ran his hand across the face of the monster and felt pity for a thing that knew nothing but how to kill. Was he the same? He told himself he wasn't, while still wondering in his own primal, beating heart.

Gathelaus put the tip of his sword to the great amber eye and said, "You're done killing."

Fiendal snorted, as if resigned to its fate.

"But I am not." He slammed the sword through the eye and into the dragon's brain.

The final scream of the dragon echoed off the canyon walls and then the beast was still. Morning's light washed over the mountains, and the others dared venture inside the cleft.

They crowded in, afraid at first that the dragon had risen again and devoured their commander. But upon seeing the dead monster with Gathelaus's sword in its eye, they moved closer and dared touch the great beast.

As Hoskuld had told Gathelaus earlier, it was a warm-blooded monster. Perhaps that was how it was able to survive in the cold of winter.

The wall wardens spoke of the wealth that such a find could bring and stories they could tell in the taverns on lonely cold nights.

Hoskuld patted Gathelaus on the back. "What can I possibly do to thank you? You're a hero, like in those legends of old. How can I repay you?"

Gathelaus stretched, took stock of his bloody garments and broken mail, and answered, "I owed you for the loss of your land's sons and daughters. Now you can build again with a new legend to tell."

"There must be something I can do?"

"I still need that drink."

Hoskuld laughed. "It can be arranged!"

FURY ɣ ɣ ɣ JAMES ALDERDICE

The wall wardens tried to hack off the head of the beast, but could get nowhere, even with a dead dragon, so they decided they would wait and let the worms do their business and come back later and take the skull back as a trophy for Hoskuld's new hall.

Gathelaus looked the monster over and examined the head. There were no marks where an axe had stove in and taken three teeth like the old rhyme had said. The jawline was flawless, as there had been nothing that could bring harm to the monster.

"Perhaps they have teeth like a shark? Forever folding in and coming in anew?" suggested Niels. He knew well what it was Gathelaus looked for. He curled back the dead lips of Fiendal, it took both hands to do it, he examined the big serrated teeth and wondered at their thickness and strength.

Gathelaus said, "There is no evidence of that. These sabers are his weapons alone and do not grow once he has lost them."

"Then what is the answer?"

"Maybe there was another, the mother. Curu-Calacht said that he saw the larger one when he was only a boy. She might have been felled with the blessed ax and lost her teeth before running back to the swamp and dying."

"So the dragons are done and gone?" asked Niels.

"Who knows for sure, considering the others we have seen far across the sea. But so far as we know, there are no more here. And that these people are free of the horror of Fiendal is what matters."

"Then, where is the axe?"

Gathelaus shrugged. "Maybe it was stuck and in her death throes, she took it to the bottom of the marsh?"

"Then maybe the cave beyond holds treasure?" Each man looked at the dark water, reluctant to swim in it any more than they had already. "But with all the death Fiendal has caused there has been no tale of him carrying off any gold or treasure, so I don't think there is a hoard."

"Perhaps so, and I have no desire to go swimming into that darkness to investigate an unlikely chance."

Hoskuld rode his horse about the fallen dragon. "What matters now is that the terror is dead. Let's ride back to Finnsburg and celebrate. This is the dawning of a new day in the land."

"You took the words right out of my mouth," said Niels.

Dahlia had just caught up to them and dismounted, making her way like an angel of the morning's light toward them.

"As I was saying," said Niels. "It will be a good thing to stay here a bit, lick our wounds and celebrate some."

Gathelaus clapped him on the shoulder. "I think there is time for that."

17. A MOTHER'S VENGEANCE

The wall wardens took the clawed arm and put a huge iron nail through the inside of the flesh beside the bone. They pounded it with hammers until it punctured through the outside of the dragon's scales and stuck it to the wood of the great pillar of Votan inside the hall. A few drops of blood ran down from the red nail and mingled with the ornate carvings in the wood that denoted the images of the old gods and their battles with the titans and monsters of eld.

To celebrate victory over the grim beast, Hoskuld ordered kegs of beer and casks of wine to be opened and shared with all. Mutton and pork that had been hidden away for fear of needing to last the winter and kept from the monster were brought forth and shared in jubilant celebration.

The skalds sang and the hall echoed with laughter and joy, more so than it had since the days when the hall was first built. At last joy returned to Hoskuld's house since the monster was dead.

Hoskuld toasted to mighty Gathelaus and praised his cunning and power in destroying the terrible curse that had ruined their land. He swore to follow Gathelaus, that he would be his most loyal vassal once he had won back the crown from cruel Vikarskeid.

Women danced and men sang, and the booming joyous music was enough to wake the deep sleeper however faraway she was lying dormant in the earth.

Brodir strummed his lute, singing, "Sari took Brodir away to warm her bed and thanked him for ending her dread. They made away after many a day, they shared a drink and then did sink into the pleasures together there, I think."

"I did no such thing," objected Sari.

Brodir, strummed a strong final flourish before saying, "It's just a song and you can't blame a man for trying to make a prophecy come true."

"Prophecy?" she asked.

"Sure, I was working the magic of song."

Sari smiled. "Well, it will take more than a song for you to warm my bed."

Brodir grinned. "Then you have but tell me what I must do, my lady," he said bowing low. "My lord, Gathelaus, is there any song I might sing in honor of your great victory?"

Gathelaus shook his head. He was sore from the struggle the night before and felt as tired as he ever had, so he toasted to Brodir and waved him off as he was shown to a comfortable room to sleep in, far away from the boisterous hall.

Brodir began the following as he did recount this many a time years later…

"The hero slayer of dreaded Fiendal, yes, mighty Gathelaus, was given the finest room lord Hoskuld had, and in a bed of white silk and warm wool, he slept dreaming of white kings that should bow to him.

"Young lovers, Dahlia and Niels did too go away to her chambers to speak privately and they did close the door and curtains to hold that magic best too.

"But those that remained in the hall were full of revelry and joy and so into the night did most fall, asleep in their cups or upon the long benches, their bellies full, and their thirst greatly quenched.

"But somewhere, something heard the din, breaking open, and yet it noticed something amiss, their child which had heretofore always been first to awake and call for silence did speak no more. The noise and throng, how it carried on, and yet no sound from the son was to be found. Curious and wondering, the sleeper did awake and crawl forth from the deep and dark lake.

"Crawling forward through the gloom and fully awaking from her long sleep, she glanced inside her lair. Her guardian was gone and yet the terrible sounds of men filled her ear. Diving back into the waters and exiting the cavern, she arose in the marsh.

"She found her son, slain, and left desecrated and foul, and she cried aloud with fear, pain and hate.

"The source of her pain was the same as that which echoed so much joy, and to them, she swore they would soon meet and be slain.

"The moon was ripe and full, ready to burst with cold light, when Fiendal's mother slithered forward to bite. Her grim purpose and pain made her slink forward with speed, determination and need.

"While sober and awake, men might have heard her heavy tread, for it was vaster and greater than awful Fiendal's dread, they did not hear the swift drumming approach of that awful gait. Thunder shook the land with each step.

"She smashed through the rude gate and went to the hall, breaking the threshold to give it her all. She saw the sleepers and men lying about, women unbuttoned and all of them dreaming happy thoughts at the expense of her loss.

"But the arm, that small two fingered arm with black claws, was enough, she tore it free from Votan's pillar with her teeth and though she used her mouth to gingerly hold the arm, the rest of her body did cause great alarm. Her tail smashed bodies and sent men flying, her feet did crush and the claws, those terrible claws, did rake and tear and break everything apart.

"She smote Votan's pillar, and smashed Hoskuld's throne, till nary a stone remained atop one another.

"The men, they woke and tried to fight, but this night their mail and swords could do not but fright. The mother, she slammed and tore and broke men's hearts and bones. She smashed the hall and when done there she took to the wall and collapsed it all to make room for her gall.

FURY ✝ ✝ ✝ JAMES ALDERDICE

"It seemed to Gathelaus that an earthquake did strike his room and he was thrown under a stone boom. The headboard did more than it was meant for, by breaking the fall of a rafter and granting a space for him to survive.

"Dahlia and Niels, they were covered in thatch and hay from the roof. They at least were free to move and see the fate of the kingdom, and wrath.

"Fiendal's mother clutched the arm in her own. The few men able, brought up their own weapons in the vainglorious attempt to strike her down, they were torn apart. Last of all was Hoskuld's favored thane, a noble one named Brotheus. He brought his war spear up to send that shaft down the gullet of the terrible monster, but when Fiendal's mother snapped that crude bit of ash, she also took brave Brotheus into her gullet and crunched his bones, letting his blood stain the flagstones of the hall. She carried away his body along with her son's arm. That hell bride of a mother knocked over the rebuilt thatch roofs, the cooking cauldrons and nightly pyres did set to blazing most all the hovels where folk did hide, until the hall came down upon the heads of those inside.

"Then before the sun began to rise, the mother of hell cried aloud in a grief-stricken roar, telling them she would stand no more, she ambled off in a sad gait, back to the mere the moat and lake. What loss, ruin, and death she did make.

"For here is where Gathelaus did know, the dawn was near darkest, that there was a field of revenge sown, and that it was ready for harvest."

18. IN THE DEPTHS OF A BLACK WELL

To the survivors of the night's attack the morning sun seemed frozen to the horizon. The dawn clung to the ground, casting chilled light along the icy land. A man could step on the hard surface leaving nary a mark on the path. Even a horse hardly left sign there, but the tracks of the terrible monster left deep imprints in the cold ground. The gigantic gait was larger than Fiendal's, by almost double. They followed the gory trail back to the marsh and surveyed the same glade from the day before.

The severed head of Brotheus did greet them at the water's edge.

Vents bubbled among the reeds of the marsh and steam wafted up like wraiths dancing along the water's edge. All was as it had been yesterday, save one thing.

Fiendal's grisly corpse was gone.

"Did the monster rise again?" gasped one of the wall wardens in horror. "Empowered in death?"

"Don't be daft," chided Bors. "The mother was much larger. She took him home to her underwater lair."

Great drag marks were furrowed deep into the mud and stones showing that his body had been moved, drug by a powerful force that took it back into the inky red fissure beyond.

"Looks like it was taken into that pool and perhaps the cavern that men guess lies behind the waterfall," said Thorne.

"Maybe there is a hoard," said Niels, "Just not the kind we wanted."

Gathelaus dropped his sword belt.

The others stared after him in wonderment as if he had gone mad.

"My lord? What are you doing?" asked Hoskuld.

"If Fiendal's mother is in there, she will be coming out and attacking your people once more. This will start all over again. Unless I do the last thing she expects and go in and destroy the monster within her very own lair."

"The most dangerous place to face a dragon is their own lair," said Bors.

Gathelaus looked at him and shrugged as he tore off his tunic.

Bors said, "I can't go with you. I'm not a good swimmer, but your sword was destroyed by Fiendal, take mine. Its name is Haftmace. It is a stout blade."

Gathelaus thanked him and took hold of the sword whose hilt was chased with gold and engraved with entwined serpents that ran down the blood groove of the silver blade.

"I'm going with you," said Thorne, as he too began to undress himself from his mail.

"And I," said Niels.

"Awful dark in there though," said Hoskuld, as he looked to Dahlia. "Maybe you could…"

She nodded and dismounted.

FURY ↟ ↟ ↟ JAMES ALDERDICE

Gathelaus wondered what Hoskuld was about to suggest his daughter do, and before he could refuse, Dahlia began to undo the golden chain which hung around her neck and held the great ruby there.

She held it out to Gathelaus. "This stone was blessed of my mother and will light your way in the dark places." She ran her hand over it just so and it began to glow. Giving off a brilliant reddish hued light, illuminating their space of the glade, despite the light of day. "My mother told me that it was the heart of an angel that fell to earth. I have no reason to doubt, considering its power."

"My thanks good lady," he said, accepting the generous gift and putting it around his own neck. "I will return it to you shortly."

"When you are in deeper darkness, the light will grow to compensate," she said.

He now wore only his sword belt, trousers, mail shirt and boots, along with the gem. "The water isn't as cold as you might expect," he said. "I think these vents and gas warm it up."

"Be careful," Dahlia said. "I've heard tell of other things that live in this marsh."

"We're going with him," said Thorne and Niels simultaneously.

Gathelaus shook his head. "Niels, stay here and keep watch."

Niels wrinkled his brow. "No, I am coming with you."

"Niels, if I don't come back, you must tell the loyalists. Only you will be believed by all."

"You're needed!" said Thorne as he laughed and smacked Niels so hard on the back he almost went face first into the marsh. Niels caught himself on his saddle and looked disappointingly after Gathelaus, who dove into the inky waters and was soon followed by Thorne and two more from his loyalist company of men, Ustainn and Dorgan.

The enchanted jewel illuminated the waters between growing stalks of a seaweed-like plant, and as they swam on, they saw a cave mouth beneath the rushing torrent of the waterfall.

Slim black shadows glided quickly between the stalks, and at once Gathelaus was aware that these were a danger. He slowed his swim to draw his sword and warn his men.

Giant eels longer than a man came whipping toward them with toothy jaws open.

Ustainn panicked and rose to the surface. He was seen by those on the shore of the marshy lake where Hoskuld had archers ready for if they could see a threat, but the eels were yet concealed from their sight.

Nipped at from multiple sides, Ustainn tossed about blindly in the water until an eel took him in the throat. Blood spewed out and Ustainn died, yet still attacked by the slimy fiends.

As one of the long black eels wrapped about the man and bit at his mail, a skilled archer loosed and hit the thing in the neck. It let go of the dead man and sunk away staining the marsh red further.

Beneath the surface, Gathelaus brought his sword up and slashed at the eels, but underwater they were swifter than eagles and nipped at his boots and legs. Two of them entwined about him, biting and squeezing his legs.

Occupied with what they thought a fine meal, Thorne shot forth his dagger and severed the eels tails. Writhing on itself, the slick monstrous things unwrapped from Gathelaus and sank.

Another eel approached from a new direction and as it came to attack Thorne, Gathelaus returned the favor and smote the thing across the head with his sword, splitting it in twain.

They surfaced beside the waterfall.

"We lost Ustainn," said Thorne, "one of the eels got him in the throat."

Gathelaus nodded grimly. "Watch my back." He filled his lungs and dove back to breach the cave and ultimate lair of the dragon.

Thorne followed closely behind, as the red gem illuminated a wide cavern that was great enough for the men to swim side by side with arms outstretched and then some. No wonder Fiendal's mother had come this way.

It was farther than they initially guessed, almost the length of the great mead hall and yet they still had found no lair, but there were air pockets trapped above so they could reclaim their breath.

"Where is Dorgan?" Gathelaus asked.

Thorne shrugged. "He was right behind me."

"The tunnel is wide enough that he may have fallen behind and become disoriented, we should fetch him."

They dove back down and searched the length of the tunnel. They found Dorgan pressed up against the ceiling of the tunnel in fright.

"An eel bit me. A small one, I killed it, but I fell behind and lost sight of your light."

"He's losing blood and will attract more of those snaky vermin," said Thorne.

"You see the light of day out there?" asked Gathelaus. A pale blue gleam beckoned like a turquoise-clad maiden a short distance away.

"Yeah, so?"

"Take him out. I'll go in and keep looking."

"By yourself?" asked Thorne. "That's madness."

"Take him out. I don't think the gods sent me here to die by dragon or eel, go on."

"Damn eels," Throne snarled in argument, but he obeyed his lord. He guided Dorgan back out to the opening of the lake.

Gathelaus pressed onward into the tunnel. The red gem did light his way, but he had to stop and catch his breath twice more as wearing even the light mail shirt and boots caused him considerable struggle swimming.

Gathelaus swam farther and deeper through the gloomy tunnel until he saw the stone ceiling lift away. He surfaced and found himself in a section of the tunnel with a vast air pocket. Farther ahead some dim light came in from high above, though this was still shrouded with creeping, unwholesome vines. A waterfall was behind him and a cleft of light far to the back of the vaulted tunnel might prove to be another exit, unless he was himself too large. That would merit investigation after the matter at hand. Farther on was a lake, and beyond that, Fiendal's body lay upon a stony strand not more than a hundred paces away.

19. THE HOARD

He warily broke the surface of the inner lake. The gem did give him light, but there was natural sunlight streaming in from above. Bright yellow pillars broke through some crevice in the rocky ceiling and cast dazzling illumination revealing a wide cavernous world.

The water dripped and fell both behind and before Gathelaus from a multitude of spots in the escarpment. A few green patches even struggled to gain nourishing light against the midnight lair.

Vents of swampy gas spewed here and there in jets of flame, giving the very impression of hell. Gathelaus remembered that no one had seen Fiendal or his mother breathing flame and that he was not now surrounded by fire-breathing dragons.

He gingerly touched a slimy bottom and strode up to the shore. Ever watchful for any sign of the dreaded hell-bride. Sighting no sign of the dragon mother, he strode from the clinging dark waters. Listening intently there was no sound beyond that of the water falling in cascades.

Fiendal's body had been dragged upon the inner lake's stony beach and arranged just so in a curious pattern, as if it were lying atop several small rounded boulders. Gathelaus could see some of the boulders beneath and wondered at their curious smoothness so alien in comparison to the jagged stones of the cave.

Worse still, the bones of both men and horses had also been taken here, looking as if they had been shattered and sucked dry of marrow. It was a hideous sight, but not unexpected in a dragon's lair.

Amidst the uneven glow of orange lights was a metallic gleam not far away. There was rusted iron and steel but some of that sparkle was purer—gold! There was a hoard of treasure things in the cave, a pile of armor, weapons, gold, and jewels to astound. He wondered how it came here. Could Fiendal have carried dead men weighted with that much gold in his teeth? Unlikely. But perhaps this had been a hidden treasure vault of Hoskuld's distant ancestors and was stolen by the dragons to make their own lair. Maybe the truth birthed legends of a dragon's greedy hoard.

There was green decay and verdigris lying atop some of the coins and items, but the true gold shone through the ancient corrosion.

As he went to investigate more of the treasure hoard, a ripple of movement at his right worried Gathelaus that perhaps Fiendal was not dead. The dragon's great muscles and ribs twitched with persistent abandon.

Horror rolled over Gathelaus like a cloud, as portions of the dead dragon's body spasmed and jerked uncontrollably. A spike tore through the scaly skin from beneath. With the sound of the ripping skin came a throaty cry, similar albeit to that which Fiendal had done so recently, but of a much higher pitch.

"By Votan's beard!" swore Gathelaus.

FURY \ \ \ JAMES ALDERDICE

A smaller, dog-sized head, yet mirroring the dead monster's own, rose, covered in gore. Then another and another in turn from various points on Fiendal's body. These were small dragonets, supping upon their dead older brother. They were not large, but despite so recently feeding, their cold yellow eyes focused hungrily on Gathelaus for a warm meal instead of cold dead meat.

Gathelaus guessed that Bors sword Haftmace, might not cut through their dragon skin, but they were small enough that he hoped he could bludgeon them into submission and skewer them through the eye. That is, if they were not preternaturally quick. Their teeth looked fearsome indeed. Razor sharp and ridged, packed tightly together like a saw blade.

They clambered out of maggoty holes in Fiendal's carcass with incredible speed, making any hope of them being engorged and sluggish disappear. They faced him side by side like a pointing trident. Three wolfish dragonets rushed forward.

Snapping spastic jaws were met with firm steel.

Gathelaus launched himself backward, with the dark lake at his back, but this ploy was short-lived as one of the dragonets willfully dove into the water to flank behind him. Here he noted that the dragonets feet were splayed with webbing between the massive clawed toes and made them fine swimmers. No wonder Fiendal and his mother laired here.

Pressing in against the remaining two, Gathelaus battered one alongside the head with the sword pommel, as the other clamped its serrated teeth on the sword with his backswing. It saved a bite on his leg, but almost stole the blade from his hand. He sheared out the edge, leaving deep gouges in the steel as the dragonet fought to keep a hold on whatever bit of this man it could.

A few of its small teeth were torn out and the thing bawled.

The third emerged from the water and rushed forward. Gathelaus drew his dagger underhanded to have a second weapon. As one of the dragonets snapped its head forward trying for a bite, Gathelaus hammered the tip of the dagger into the back of its skull. The point bit in almost an inch between the scales and the dragon cried out in pain. It jerked its head back, stealing the dagger from Gathelaus's hand.

The other two quickly advanced, snapping their terrible jaws. Gathelaus took a chance and tried to slam a sword down the gullet of the nearest one, expecting the dragonet to clamp down and try and take it. This time however, it closed its mouth and tried to drive in beneath the blade.

Gathelaus was forced back against the dead body of Fiendal, nearly tripping over the dead dragon's snout.

The wounded dragonet with the dagger still stuck in the top of its skull was running far about over the stony island, bawling out in crazed pain.

Somewhere, its cry was answered by a thunderous mother.

A dragonet snapped at Gathelaus's boot, and he kicked the monster in the face. Once its head was turned, Gathelaus brought the sword up and sent the tip into its eye. The dragonet froze, stricken, its tail snapping out straight. It fell dead.

Its brother had no problems coming in for the kill. The vicious claws upon its feet tore and swiped at Gathelaus as he scrambled away.

Attempting a similar feint with this dragonet, he kicked at its head to make for a more conducive killing stroke, but it was persistent, taking the blows across its snout and coming on, thoroughly enraged.

Gathelaus slammed the tip of the sword at the dragonet's open mouth, but it turned its head at the last second and the sword tip caught it in the nostril. The sword Haftmace slid forward and he wondered if he might reach its brain and slay the thing.

It took titanic effort as Gathelaus pushed, and the blade slid along its upper jaw and skull. The dragonet made a ghastly sound, gagging on the steel as it was slowly slain. Once the sword reached almost to the hilt and the blade was all the way back, the dragonet at last went still.

The one with the dagger sticking out of its skull came forward snapping in a rage.

Gathelaus tried to withdraw the sword, but as he tugged, the blade was held tight in the skull of the other. He was bowled over by the crazed dragonet. It snapped and clawed at him madly while also pinning him to the ground with one of its terrible feet. Claws ripped into his flesh. The mouth snapped perilously close. He had no time for any other weapon but what lay at hand.

Rounded stones. He picked one up and as the dragonet snapped at him, he hammered the dagger pommel like a nail until it pierced the brain of the dragonet. Even as it fell dead on its side, it continued to strike out with its clawed feet and wailed, not unlike a chicken with its head cut off. Gathelaus had learned as a boy to hang birds upside down before butchering them, but how would you hang a two-hundred-pound snapping dragonet upside down?

The last to die let out a terrible squall and this was again answered by the mother from deeper in the cavern.

One step. Two steps. The heavy tread reverberated through the cavern. She was getting closer.

The sound echoed chaotically through the massive cave and over the lake. It was impossible to tell which direction she was coming from. He spun about, ever watchful, but dark shadows held the lower walls in thrall.

He placed a foot on the dead dragonet's head and tried to leverage his sword free from the monstrous prison. The blade of Haftmace snapped at the hilt.

"Damn," gasped Gathelaus.

20. RETURN OF THE KING

The three dragonets had been hard enough to kill, now his blade was lodged in the skull of one, never to be retrieved.

A roar like thunder sounded from over the black lake and he still could not tell from which direction it had originated.

Gathelaus guessed the she dragon was maddened that there was no reply from any of her brood. She had wrought terrible vengeance on the hall for the loss of Fiendal, what would she now do to him and the whole of Finnsburg for the death of these three dragonets? He guessed it would be swift, as wild things don't torture like a man can, nor drag out their responses, but going down the gullet of a dragon was not anything he wished to experience either.

He needed a weapon. He had only his dagger now. There was armor within the stack of hoarded things, perhaps there was something there he could use.

Hurrying to the pile of rusted armor, he threw scattered helms and breastplates about, looking for anything useful.

The roar sounded again like thunder, hard and intense. It echoed throughout the cavernous chamber and Gathelaus wondered if the men outside in the marsh could not hear her call reverberating and shaking through the earth itself.

There was a sword, ancient of days, with a caking of verdigris down the blade and hilt. It was a very long sword as if forged for giants or titans. He drew it from the sheath and knocked off a coat of rusted flakes. There was fine workmanship here, gold inlaid upon the wide forked guard and basket, but could it do the job?

Glancing over his shoulder, it seemed for a moment as if the entire wall of the cavern fell at him. She came up from the dark waters from some other unknown fork and, sighting her dead brood, went mad with crippling rage, snapping and gnashing at Gathelaus in a fury.

He dodged away as the mighty tramp of the dragon mother slammed into the ground where he had just stood. Those great claws broke the rounded river stones into gravel. The tail lashed out and he flew to the ground beneath that awful thunderbolt. But worse was her voice, that dreadful roar of doom. It deafened Gathelaus.

She had lost him in the moment and wheeled about the strand bemoaning her dead children. She nudged at the three dragonets, and Gathelaus swore that her eyes turned a deeper, ruddier color.

Facing off against Fiendal's mother seemed an incredible feat. But he had to try. He gave the war cry and slammed the blade at the great wyrm's belly.

His sword did nothing against her. The ancient blade folded over on itself with a last gasp of rusted dust. He dropped the useless thing to scramble for cover, diving beneath the shadow of Fiendal's own leg.

The great she-dragon sniffed the air, then nudged at Fiendal's corpse, though Gathelaus was on the opposite side.

She placed a foot upon Fiendal and roared once more. She surely recognized his scent as that of the being that had dared take her son's arm, her son's life.

Racing back around the corpse, she pushed it aside, revealing Gathelaus's hiding place. He launched up and away as her swift snapping movements did not allow for him to try the same tactic against the larger dragon, he was not sure that even if he could reach her arm, nor would he have the strength to break it. Her being twice as large as Fiendal.

Then he saw the awful scar across her lip and jaw—what did the old rhyme say? That *she had been bested by the blessed axe of the wolf witch, Halla*. A Pictish sorcerous perhaps? And therefore, perhaps there was a weapon here that could cut her.

The tail swung out and just the tip caught Gathelaus across the chest and sent him sailing away.

Knocked back into the hoard, his hand found the haft of the magical axe. Amazed at his good fortune, he strained to pull the thing free as the head was buried beneath a pile of hoard accruements.

It was too heavily laden beneath gold coins and silver arm rings, along with the bones of dead kings and cold knighted bones.

Fiendal's mother slammed a foot down atop the hoard, nearly taking Gathelaus's head off. The wind from her taloned foot whistled past his ear. He moved.

Bolting back into the dark of the cavern, the glow of the red gem gave away his position despite the dragon seeming to have poor vision.

The deafening monster charged toward the red light and in desperation, Gathelaus tore the glowing gem from his neck and flung it into the lake behind him. He moved aside a few paces to avoid the charging crash of the dragon. It raced past him and dove into the black lake in pursuit of the glowing stone that soon sank from view.

Running back to the hoard pile, Gathelaus tossed away the trash and wealth of ages past. He strove to free the axe, trusting it would be of some use against the awful monster.

The axe head was a massive double blade. It was almost black and seemed a curious, crude workmanship of iron, but that there was no rust, even in this wet environment, was something indeed. Almost invisible, all along the sweeping edge were a series of runes of a make that Gathelaus could not read or identify. Could they be of a lost Pictish language? They had no writing that he was aware of, but that certainly didn't mean one didn't exist at least for their sorcerers and shamans. The axe head was crafted tightly onto what seemed a stout piece of oak, but it was ancient, and he wondered a moment if the wood would hold against savage blows, even if the edge could cut a dragon's hide.

Fiendal's mother had not risen from the lake yet, but he guessed she would be back at any moment. He had an idea.

He went to Fiendal's corpse. Where the dragonets had eaten and broke free, the skin was peeled back and ripped.

He took hold of a piece of the dragon's steely skin and pulled. A strip tore free. He quickly wrapped this about the haft of the axe, then took a second piece and then a third until the whole of the axe was wrapped tight with dragon skin cords.

The black lake boiled as a leviathan of evil arose.

Fiendal's mother erupted from the hellish bottom, holding the glowing red gem with her tongue. Her ruddy eyes fixed upon Gathelaus. She spat the gem onto the piled hoard as she strode forth.

Gathelaus could see now that she bore a terrible scar along her lower jaw and in that place, was missing several of her enormous teeth.

"If only Sigurd had finished you in those days," he said aloud. "But you escaped him and slept, licking your wounds and giving forth a new brood of monsters."

The dragon gave a crocodilian growl that echoed off the cavern walls.

"This ends here," he said.

FURY ↯ ↯ ↯ JAMES ALDERDICE

The great dragon roared her challenge and stepped forth on those two great legs, like mighty oaks, crushing helms and armor beneath its fabled tread.

Gathelaus held the axe at the ready, timing his strike for all the power he could throw behind it and still move if it failed.

One step closer. Two steps. The dragon's mouth, a throne of sworded teeth, opened wide and reached to take him into her jaws.

Gathelaus slammed the axe blade into her mouth and cracked the bottom jaw in half.

Fiendal's mother shrieked. This thing had cut her. Did she remember this axe? Did she remember Sigurd taking several of her teeth? She backed away, shaking her head as a dizzying amount of blue-black blood rained down.

Bold runes glowed upon that axe head as if they drank in her blood. They worked their old magic against the primal foe. Drawing the axe head back, Gathelaus swung again and caught the now retreating monster in the ribs. Again, the runes along the edge glowed even brighter as if they stole away the dragon's very life essence.

The dragon crashed backward over her own tail as Gathelaus charged forth and slammed the axe head deep into her brain, slaying the great dragon.

The runes glowed as if they were heated in a forge, turning almost white hot. But as the dragon died, the runes, too, did fade.

Gathelaus pondered if this mighty weapon shouldn't be his own now, but then he gave pause as a curious sizzling sound made him realize that the weapon, now having fulfilled the measure of its enchantment, was done. The black iron sizzled and crumbled everywhere the dragon's blood had touched. Which was almost every shred of it. Finally, only the dragon skin wrapped handle was left, but as Gathelaus picked it up, the wooden shaft fell apart in his hands, as if it were but dust held together beneath dragon skin.

Movement behind had him wheeling to fight whatever new foe revealed itself. But it was only Thorne.

He shook his head in grinning disbelief. "This is why you are my king!" He proclaimed.

"Eh?"

Thorne laughed, slapped Gathelaus on the shoulder, and looked him in the eyes. "I followed a brave man into a cavern, but only a true king could slay that monster single handed. You're a legend you are."

Gathelaus knelt and picked up Dahlia's gem from where Fiendal's mother had cast it back into the hoard.

Thorne glanced about the chamber. He saw the three dragonets. "And those? You are a legend!"

"Let's go back. I'm tired," said Gathelaus. "I'll hardly be able to swim back on my own.

"What of this wealth here?" asked Thorne, pointing at even just the fraction of the hoard he could see.

Gathelaus wondered. "We'll take back whatever we can still swim with. No wait, I think there might be another exit, yonder." They picked up whatever they could carry. Thorne filling a helm full of gold coins for each of them.

Gathelaus led toward the tunnel where he had seen a flash of daylight. Sure enough, there was an opening in the rock shrouded by vegetation. It was almost too small for the men to pass through, but they did, and found themselves a good way from the others in the marsh who awaited their return.

Gathelaus returned Dahlia's magical gem and awarded most of the coin to Hoskuld in hopes he could rebuild and bring more folk back to his hamlet as well as buy more sheep and livestock that the farmers so desperately needed.

Then, with a bittersweet farewell between Niels and Dahlia, they prepared for their journey to reclaim the lost kingdom.

"I will return for you," said Niels.

Dahlia gave him a coy smile and wrapped her own crimson scarf about his neck. "You best be worthy of my name and title."

"I shall do my best, good lady," he said, as she kissed his cheek.

FURY ↟ ↟ ↟ JAMES ALDERDICE
EPILOGUE: TO THE CROWN

The bright morning sun was ahead of them on the road and as they trotted along, full of hope and gaining the first mile, they noticed a pair of men waiting for them at the crossroads.

"Did you have word for more loyalists to join us?" asked Gathelaus.

Niels shook his head. "No. Not that there are that many more loyalists anyway. But I was discreet."

As they drew near, Gathelaus recognized both men. Tarbona, chief of the huntsmen, and Dagoo, his Pictish tracker.

"Not the welcome I expected," said Gathelaus. He glanced back and forth along the road. Besides the waybill etched crookedly against the sun, there was no shade nor cover here. Nowhere for more huntsmen to hide that might be supporting Tarbona's brazen stance with a trap. "Is your ambush any larger or are you surrendering?"

Tarbona scowled. "You cost me a lot of men."

"That's the business you're in. You've gotta expect some risks."

Tarbona nodded. "Risks I can expect, but not disgrace and dishonor. You went below the belt."

"Me? You tried to ambush me in a little fishing village. All is fair in war. Perhaps you're not as experienced at this sort of thing as you ought to be," said Gathelaus, with a wicked grin.

"You set sorcery on me. A doom of a werewolf and a dragon. Is that how an honorable man fights?"

Gathelaus laughed. "You are a backstabbing huntsman serving a tyrant of a king. What honor?"

Tarbona was not goaded to answer that question but continued with his own debate. "I know you pride yourself as honorable, and so I challenge you to a duel. I must win back my dignity."

Gathelaus held back a chuckle. "Leader of the huntsmen. Backstabbers and way-layers by night, and you talk of honor to me?"

"I have always lived by the code and done what I was contracted to do," snapped Tarbona. "I've done no truck with witches or warlocks. Do you stand by my insult?"

"Ah, now we have the truth of the matter. You accepted money for a job you didn't finish?" taunted Gathelaus.

Tarbona slowly nodded. "Hawkwood paid me to do a job. I'll see your skull decorate the parapet in Hellainik."

"You haven't collected yet."

Tarbona stepped away from the signposts and threw back his cloak, revealing a fine sword hilt at his side. "Fight me. And hold your men to not interfere if I win, and they will be free to go."

"Free to go?" laughed Thorne.

Gathelaus held up a hand, calling for silence. "If Tarbona defeats me, nowhere in Vjorn would remain safe for you. He is bargaining safe passage away, *if* he can win."

FURY \ \ \ JAMES ALDERDICE

Tarbona drew his long-curved sword and swung it in a great kata before himself. The sun caught on the razored edge and dazzled the eye.

Gathelaus nodded and dismounted. "You look as if you have studied the way of the bushi."

"I have," answered Tarbona. "Under master Tengow Uyama. I have learned much from the masters in the Sen-Toku empire."

"Good," was Gathelaus's simple answer. "So have I." He stepped forward, keeping his own blade sheathed.

Tarbona cocked his head and re-sheathed his blade. Both men drew near to one another until they were only three paces apart.

Eyes bore into one another and hands remained at their sides.

This was the strangest duel any of Gathelaus's men had ever seen. Several times they looked to one another in wonderment. One whispered to Niels, "Is he bewitched?"

Niels shushed him, never taking his eyes from his lord's hands.

Only Dagoo, the Pictish tracker, remained unperplexed. He had a lazy way of sitting and watching upon his rough saddle. He chewed on a long sprout of wheat.

Gathelaus and Tarbona remained frozen in place.

Then finally, Tarbona's right hand made a move for his hilt.

Faster than the eye could follow, Gathelaus's left hand shot forth clutching his own hilt and drawing it up underhanded, while the right hand pushed the end of the long blade into Tarbona's chest and out the back.

A great gout of blood shot from Tarbona's exposed heart like a crimson waterfall. It gushed and Tarbona stood paralyzed for a moment, lost in time before collapsing at Gathelaus's feet.

Niels, Thorne, and the rest cheered.

"Hush," commanded Gathelaus. "He deserves a dignified death with silence."

The men looked to one another in confusion.

Dagoo hopped down from his saddle and, bowing before Gathelaus, picked up Tarbona's corpse by the armpits and drug him back only a few feet to a shallow pit that had recently been dug.

"Who prepared that?" asked Gathelaus.

"Dagoo did," said Dagoo. "Dagoo tell old master, pit would be for you. Dagoo say it only right. He say he would take only your head but allow your body to be buried here."

Gathelaus looked at the little man curiously. "Old master?"

Dagoo thumped his chest and then pointed at Gathelaus. "Yes, you new master."

"You think I want your service?" asked Gathelaus.

"Dagoo great tracker. Dagoo talk to spirits, know that you will win back kingdom. Must serve you now. Only safe place in kingdom is under your banner."

"You knew I would win against Tarbona or my kingdom?"

"Dagoo knows you will win. Both," said Dagoo with a shrug. "But Dagoo cannot tell old master that. Dagoo could not rob him of hope."

"Of course not," said Gathelaus.

Dagoo rapidly threw a few spades of dirt over Tarbona. "Must not ride to Hellainik yet," he said shaking his head. "Hawkwood have big trap for you on the outskirts of city."

"No one knew we came this way," said Niels.

"How do you know this Dagoo?" asked Gathelaus.

The Pict scratched at his scalp. "Spirits tell Dagoo many things if he asks the right questions. Tarbona wanted to know these things for return trip with your head. He did not want anyone to steal the glory."

"Which way do you think I should go to win back my kingdom?"

Dagoo shrugged. "All Dagoo has asked yet is where Dagoo will ride with you next." He finished another shovel full atop Tarbona and stowed his spade.

"Where is that?"

Dagoo pointed far to the east. "Spirits say you must get many fighting men from Marence and Hawkton. You need many more men to face Vikarskeid again. It will take army to win back kingdom, just like when you first took it."

Gathelaus looked to his dubious men. He pondered the words of the Pict in his mind and his gut. He trusted his heart telling him what the strange man said was so. "I think he speaks true. It won't hurt for a bit of caution as well as gaining some good men to retake the kingdom."

Niels asked, "So where are we going?"

"To Marence and the cities of the peninsula to gain an army!" shouted Gathelaus, drawing his sword and leading his men forward.

Continued in **WRATH**

If you enjoyed this book, please leave a review.

ABOUT THE AUTHOR:

James Alderdice aka David J. West writes dark fantasy and weird westerns because the voices in his head won't quiet until someone else can hear them. He is a great fan of sword & sorcery, ghosts and lost ruins, so of course he lives in Utah in with his wife and children.

You can visit him online at:

https://www.jamesalderdice.com/

http://david-j-west.blogspot.com/

https://twitter.com/David_JWest